WELCOME TO STRANGE PLANET!

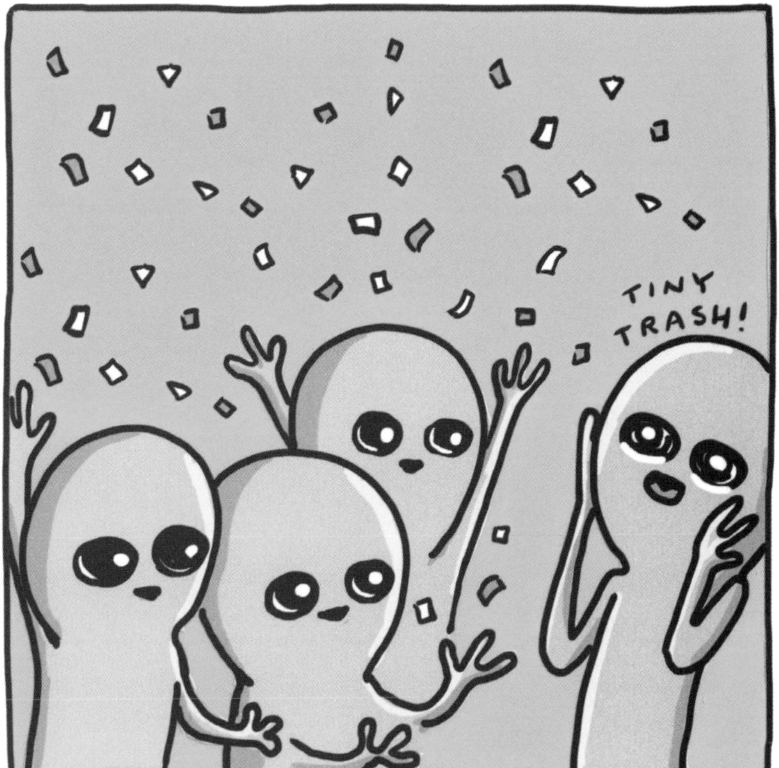
TINY TRASH!

THIS BOOK IS MADE FOR BEINGS
WHO LIKE TO SIT AND THINK

BEINGS WHO EAT FOOD
AND BEINGS WHO DRINK DRINKS

BEINGS WHO LIKE PUZZLES
AND WRITING WORDS IN SPACES

BEINGS WITH EMOTIONS
WHO CAN MAKE EXPRESSIVE FACES.

STRANGE PLANET

ACTIVITY BOOK

NATHAN W PYLE

HARPER
An Imprint of HarperCollins Publishers

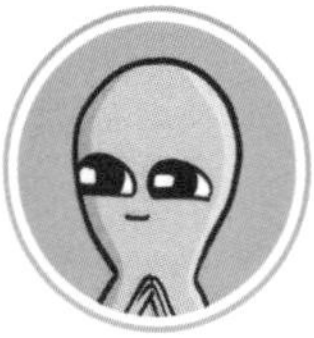

STRANGE PLANET ACTIVITY BOOK

 FOR INFORMATION ADDRESS HARPERCOLLINS CHILDREN'S BOOKS, A DIVISION OF HARPERCOLLINS PUBLISHERS, 195 BROADWAY, NEW YORK, NY 10007.
WWW.HARPERCOLLINSCHILDRENS.COM

ISBN 978-0-06-304975-8

TYPOGRAPHY BY NATHAN W. PYLE
DESIGN AND LAYOUT BY JESSICA NORDSKOG
PRODUCTION MANAGEMENT BY STONESONG
21 22 23 24 25 PC/WOR 10 9 8 7 6 5 4 3 2 1
FIRST EDITION

SO IF YOU ARE A BEING
(AND I'M CERTAIN THAT YOU ARE),

AND IF YOU'RE ON A PLANET
THAT IS CIRCLING A STAR,

IF YOU POSSESS A BRAIN
(I'M VERY CERTAIN THAT YOU DO),

THEN IT'S EASY TO DEDUCE THAT YES,
THIS BOOK IS MADE FOR YOU!

ALL ABOUT YOU!

WHAT DO YOU CALL YOURSELF?

Jame / J / Jamie

HOW MANY REVOLUTIONS AROUND THE NEAREST STAR HAVE YOU MADE?

25

HOW MANY MOUTH STONES DO YOU HAVE?

all

HOW MANY MOUTH STONES HAVE YOU LOST?

all

WILL THE MAGICAL MOUTH STONE BEING VISIT TONIGHT?

DO ANY CREATURES OR OTHER BEINGS LIVE WITH YOU?

 YES (CIRCLE ONE) NO

IF SO, WHAT ARE THEY CALLED?

Abbie + nellie

WHAT TIME DO YOU SINK INTO YOUR REST SLAB AND EXIT TO BEGIN THE DAY?

10PM-12AM

WHO IS YOUR FAVORITE COMPANION?

Jacob

MATCH EACH IMAGE TO A DESCRIPTION BELOW.

LIFEGIVER AND
OFFSPRING

VIBRATING CREATURE

YELLING CREATURE

SUPER LIFEGIVERS

RELOCATED ORGANISM

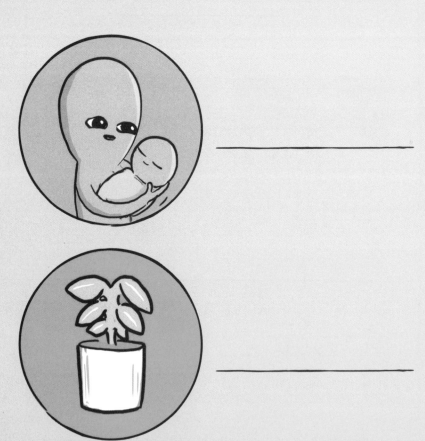

_____

_____

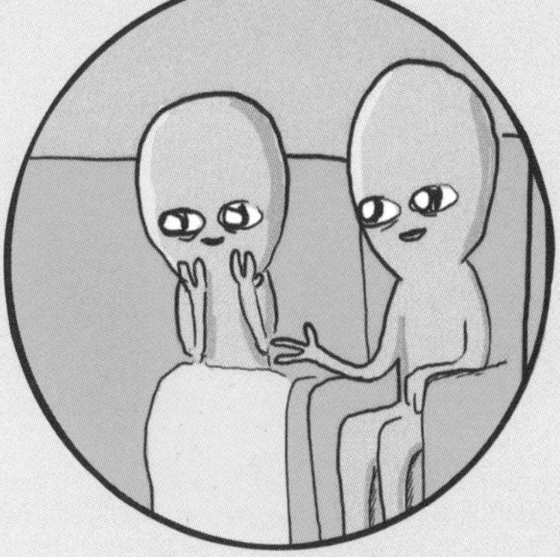

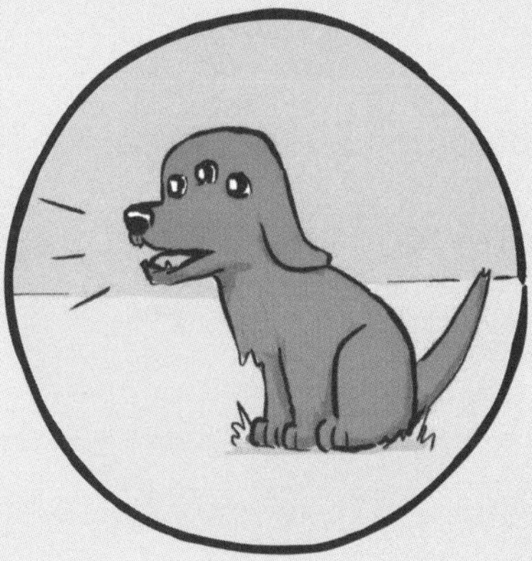

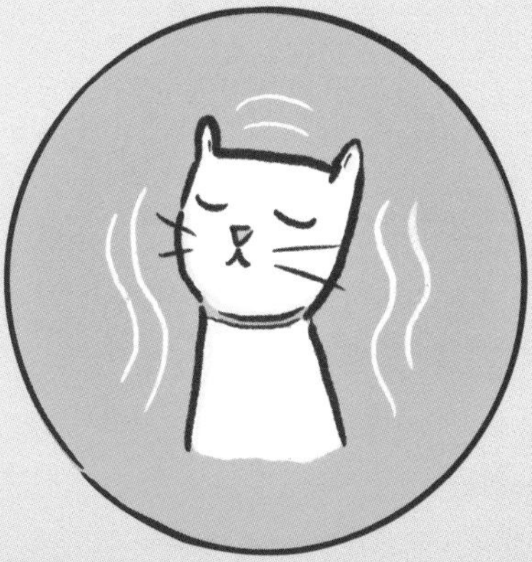

HOW TO DRAW BEINGS!

DRAW A BEING IN THE PINK BOX.

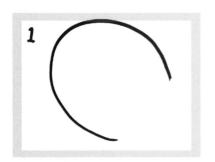

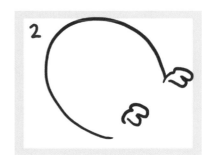

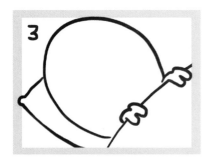

YOUR LINES DO NOT HAVE TO BE PERFECT!
MINE NEVER ARE!

CRISS-CROSS PUZZLE

START YOUR DAY WITH NOURISHMENT BY FILLING IN THE CRISS-CROSSWORD.

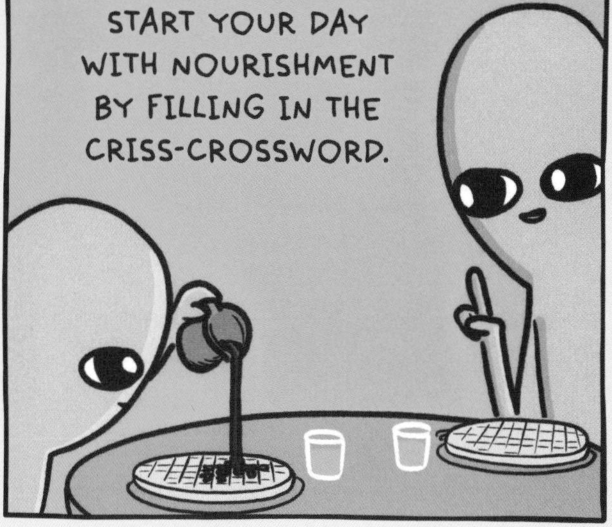

1 waffle
2 knives
3 for
4 coffee
5 syrup

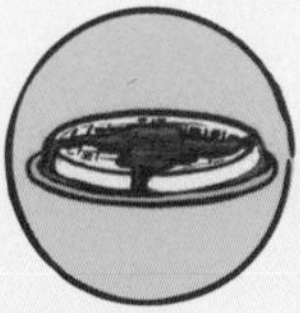

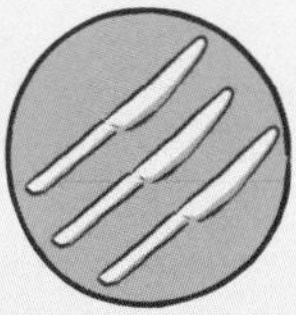

ACROSS

1. CRISS-CROSS FLOPPER
2. SLICERS

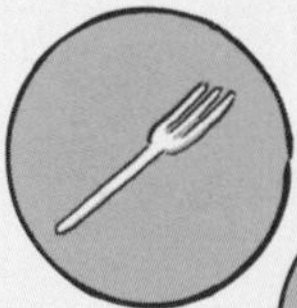

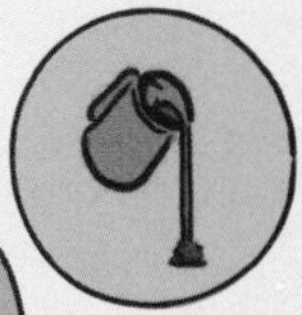

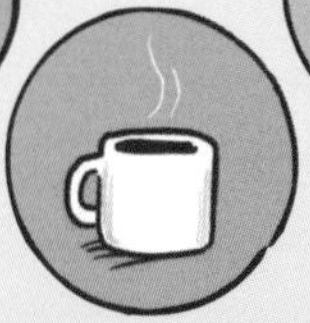

DOWN

3. STABBER
4. JITTER LIQUID
5. SWEET SAUCE

BRUSH MOUTH STONES

FILL IN THE BLANKS WITH
WORDS FROM THE BANK TO
MAKE A MELODY THAT RHYMES.

SHINE	STONES
SHRED	RECLINE
BONES	HEAD

WE NEED OUR STONES
TO BITE AND _____,
THIS KEEPS THEM FIRMLY
IN OUR _____

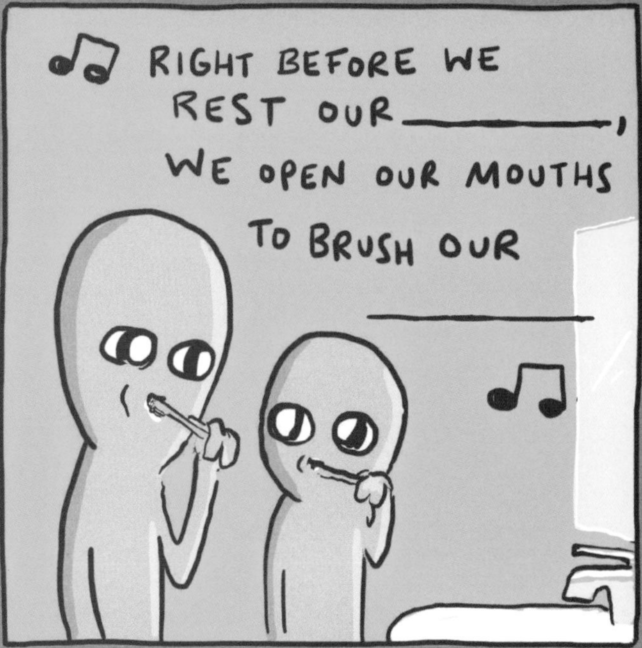
RIGHT BEFORE WE REST OUR ________, WE OPEN OUR MOUTHS TO BRUSH OUR ________

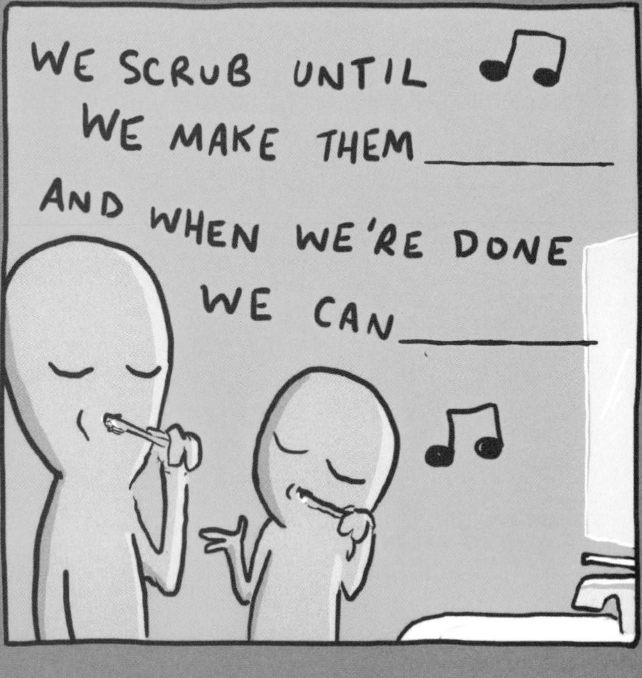
WE SCRUB UNTIL WE MAKE THEM ________
AND WHEN WE'RE DONE WE CAN ________

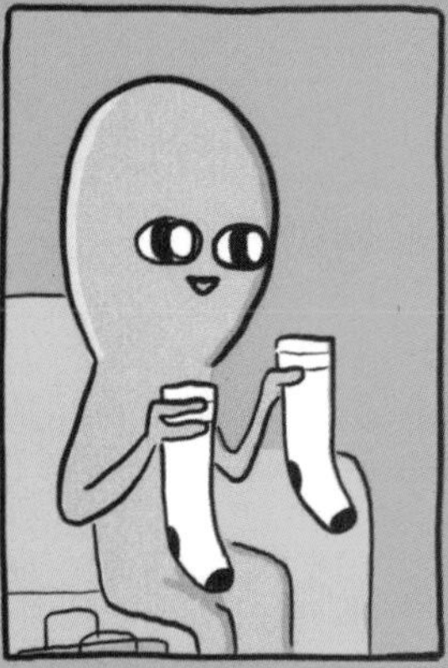

FIND FOOT FABRIC TUBES

CIRCLE THE TWO SETS OF FOOT FABRIC TUBES THAT ARE DIFFERENT FROM THE REST.

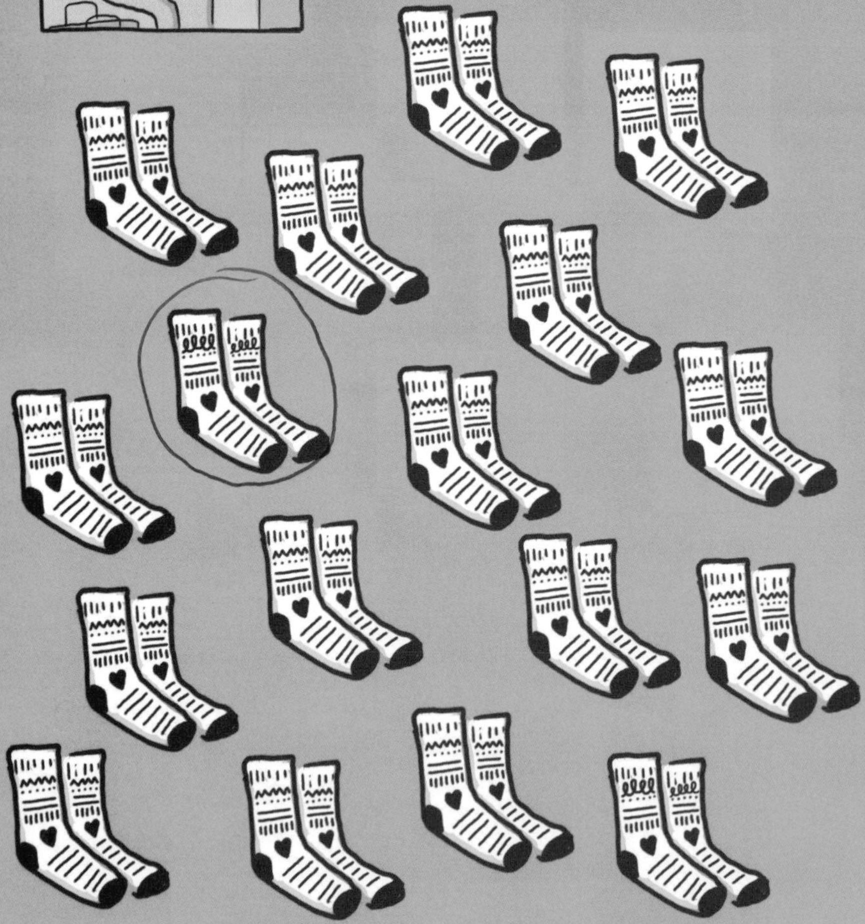

PACK YOUR BEHIND-BAG

DRAW LINES CONNECTING THE ITEMS
YOU NEED FOR THE LEARNING CHAMBER.
AVOID NON-LEARNING ITEMS!

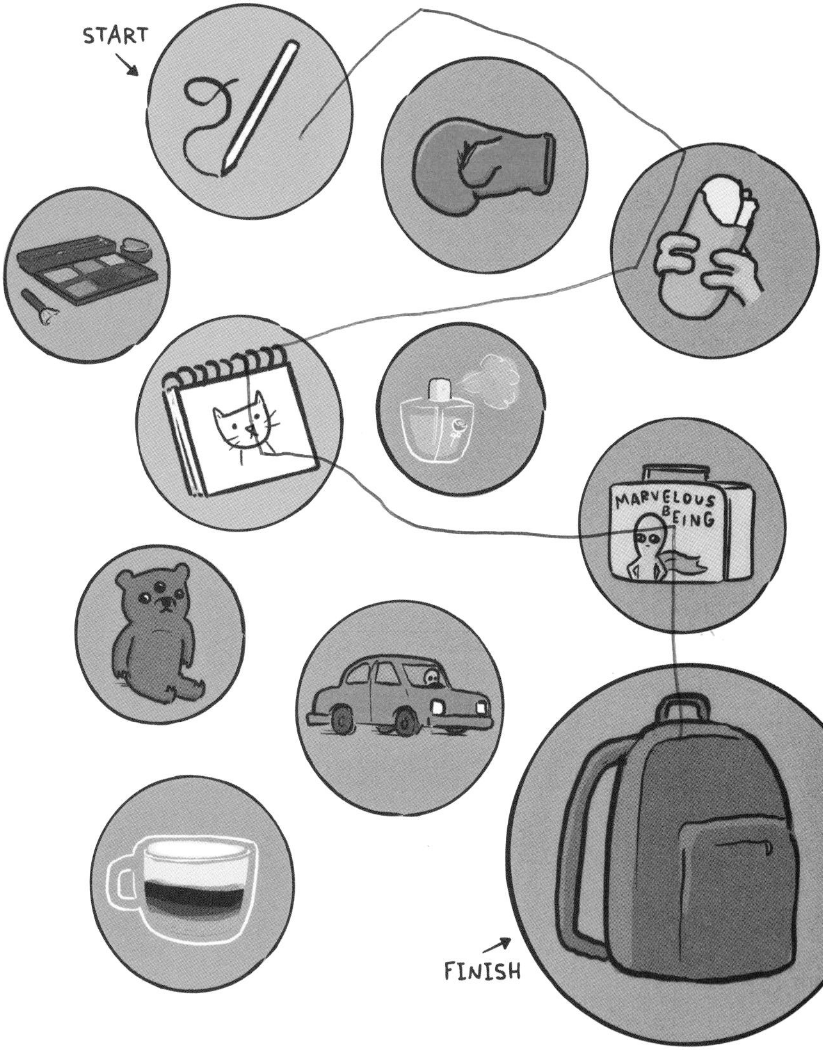
START
MARVELOUS BEING
FINISH

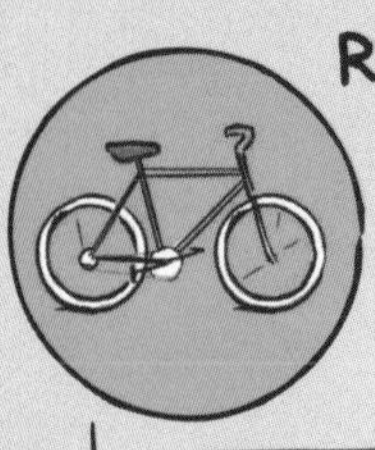

RIDE YOUR TWO-WHEEL FOOT PUSHER TO THE LEARNING CHAMBER.

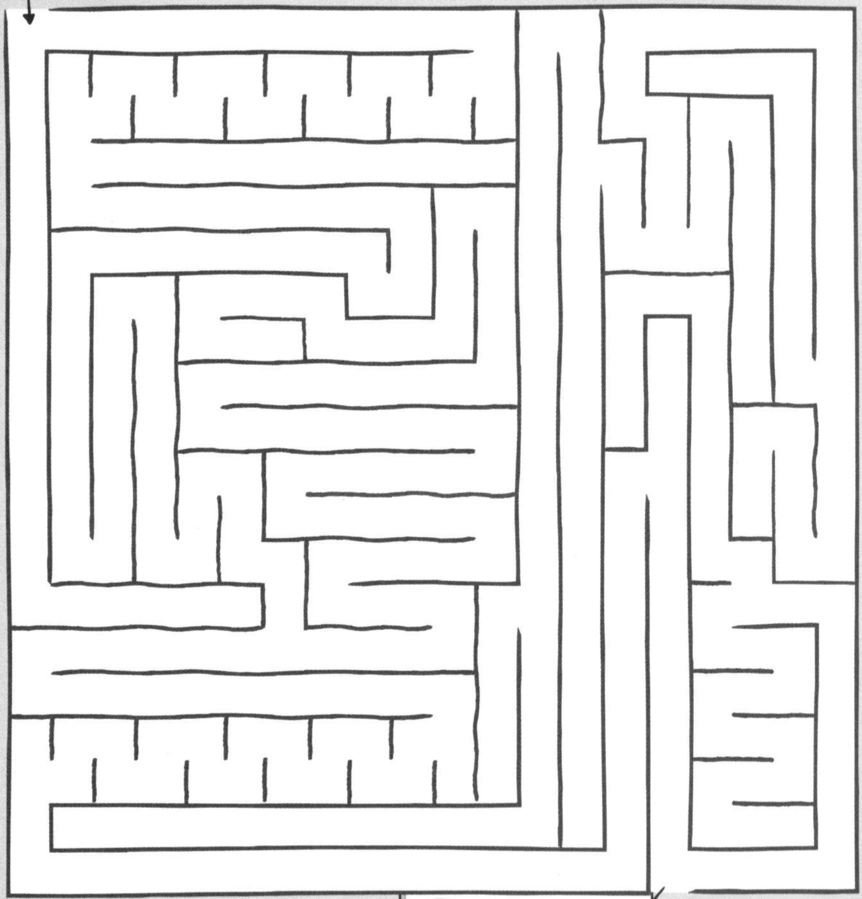

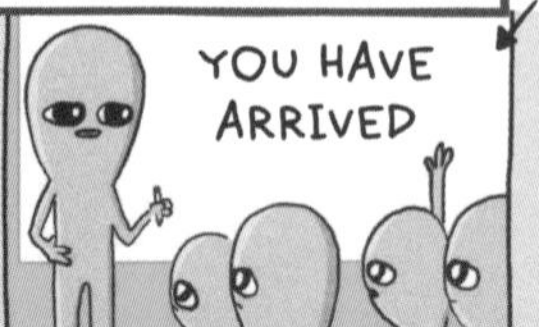
YOU HAVE ARRIVED

CONNECT THE DOTS TO FIND YOUR TWO-WHEEL FOOT PUSHER.

WHO IS THE LONGEST BEING?

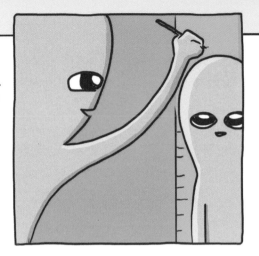

CONVERT INCHES TO FEET TO FIND THE LONGEST BEING.

48" _____

42" _____

54" _____

HOW MANY INCHES LONG ARE YOU?

_____

12 INCHES = 1 FOOT

THE POWER OF 10

FILL IN THE BLANKS TO COMPLETE THE NUMBER PATTERNS.

10 20 30 40 50 60

90 80 70 60 50 40

10 20 40 80 160 320

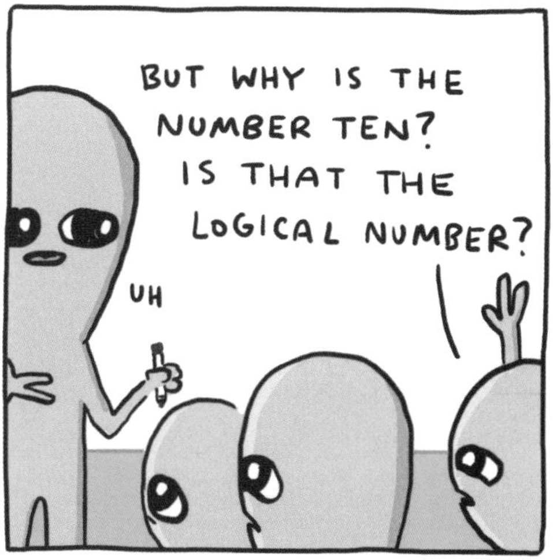
BUT WHY IS THE NUMBER TEN? IS THAT THE LOGICAL NUMBER?
UH

LET'S CONSUME SOME SUSTENANCE!

FIND AND CIRCLE THE FOLLOWING WORDS IN THE SUSTENANCE SEARCH.

CREAMY FLUID

EXPLODING GRAINS

ENERGY ROD

DOUGHSLICE

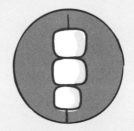

SWEET CUSHIONS

SPRINKLED MINERALS

LEAFBUCKET

FROZEN THICKNESS

L T T I E Q G R D F S C Y D
C E L I F B N D I O N W M R
E X A Z M M B S U L O J D S
O P E F E A D S L O I V Q L
S L N U B G C T F U H G J A
S O E L X U H C Y E S E U R
E D R E J Y C P M H U M Z E
N I G A M A M K A S C B F N
K N Y E Y E D A E D T Y W I
C G R B C Z U U R T E W Y M
I G O U R I H Y C C E I A D
H R D C H A L Z E G W T O E
T A W K X A Y S V R S R M L
N I S E S Z M N H G Y F G K
E N J T O U L U I G O G T N
Z S R W G V Q Y R Q U V B I
O V F F G O S E O L Z O B R
R K G L O C N J T H Y J D P
F W Z V F E I G G B I Y A S

TRANSLATOR!

DRAW A LINE TO CONNECT THE STRANGE PLANET WORDS TO THEIR CORRESPONDING IMAGES.

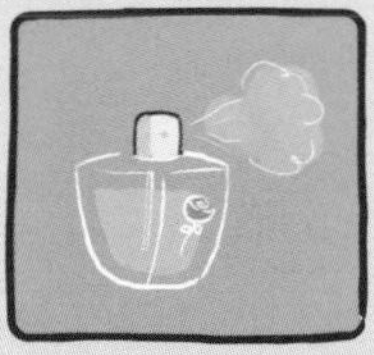

LIVING ORGANISM

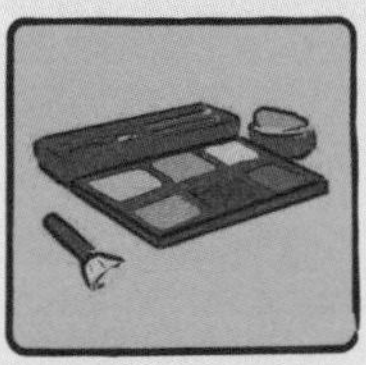

FOOT-ORB

FLYING CREATURE

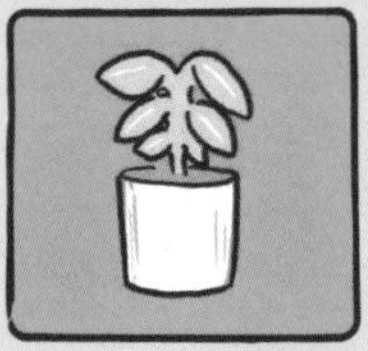

FACIAL TOPOGRAPHY KIT

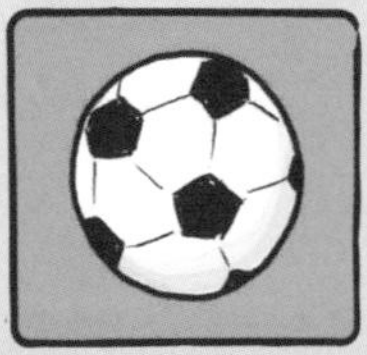

PLANT SCENT LIQUID

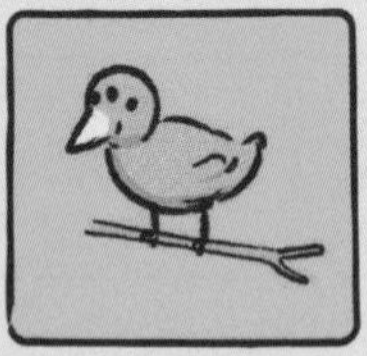

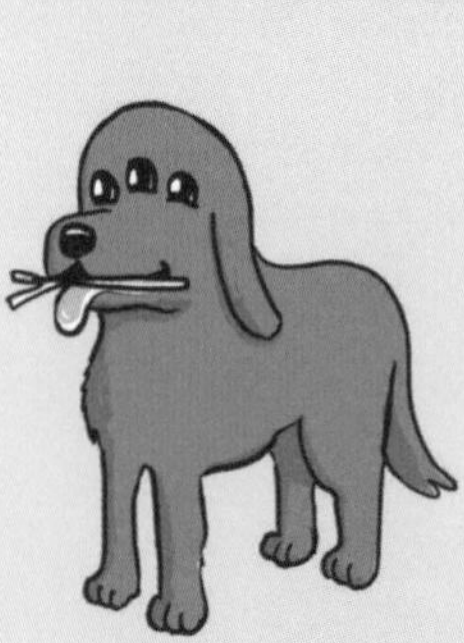

NOW CREATE YOUR OWN STRANGE PLANET PHRASE FOR "DOG":

REST SLAB CHAMBER

CREATE A LOW-DETAIL RENDERING
OF YOUR REST SLAB CHAMBER.

CREATE 10 WORDS
USING LETTERS FROM THE PHRASE
"IMAGINE PLEASANT NONSENSE."

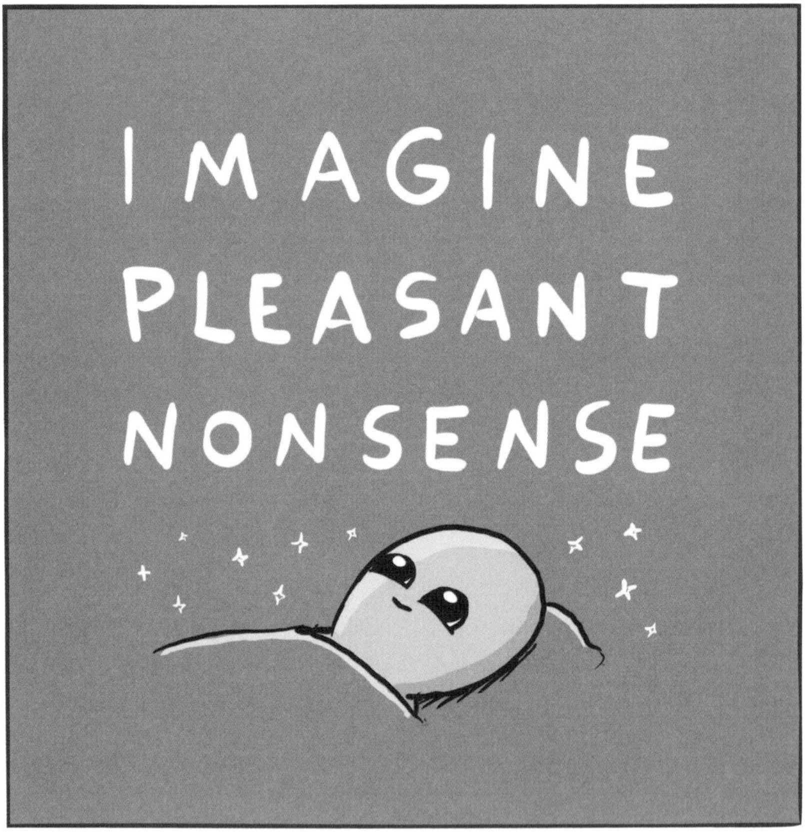
IMAGINE
PLEASANT
NONSENSE

THE FIRST ONE IS
DONE FOR YOU!

1 SLEEPING _____

2 _____

3 _____

4 _____

5 _____

6 _____

7 _____

8 _____

9 _____

10 _____

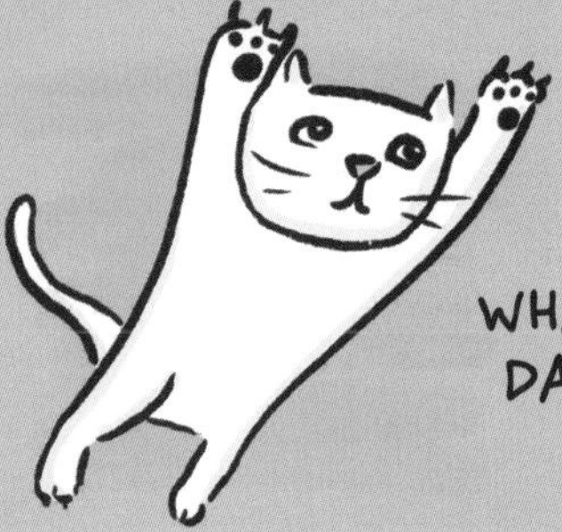

ERRATIC CREATURE SEARCH

WHAT DOES YOUR CREATURE DO ALL DAY? FIND WORDS IN THE SEARCH.

VIBRATE	LICK	CLIMB
SNEAK	NAP	PLOP
SHOVE	OBSERVE	HIDE
	SCRITCHSCRATCH	

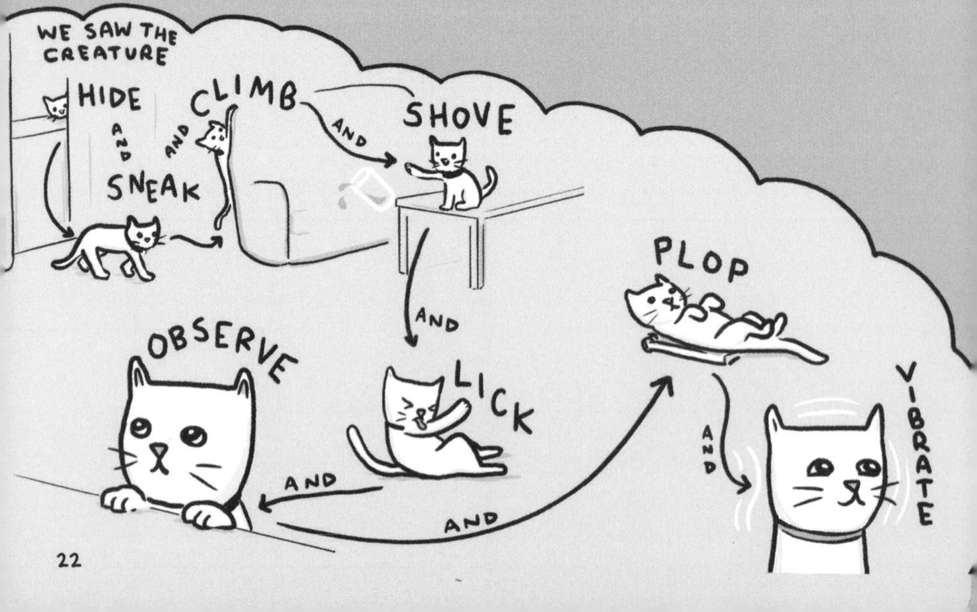
WE SAW THE CREATURE
HIDE
AND
SNEAK
AND
CLIMB
AND
SHOVE
AND
LICK
AND
OBSERVE
AND
PLOP
AND
VIBRATE

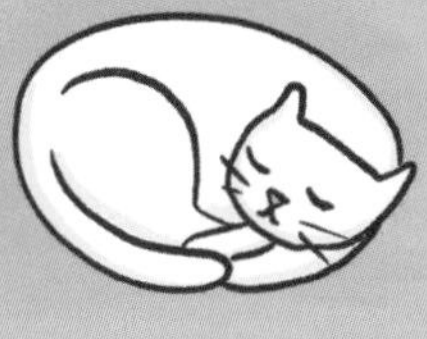

H	O	F	I	H	B	B	R	Q	X	B	H
C	L	V	T	N	E	M	R	S	M	V	O
T	T	J	N	E	V	I	G	P	U	L	A
A	W	B	A	S	O	L	B	U	S	M	X
R	E	L	P	Z	H	C	I	T	X	P	L
C	K	O	V	U	S	V	Y	D	I	O	D
S	M	A	S	X	O	G	D	Q	P	K	W
H	T	I	E	H	O	K	J	T	C	A	E
C	H	V	T	N	B	D	J	I	D	Y	O
T	B	T	X	U	S	B	L	J	G	C	J
I	P	C	S	T	E	X	R	A	Q	G	M
R	R	F	E	Q	R	T	B	O	Y	E	P
C	M	Y	M	T	V	C	A	T	N	H	C
S	U	H	E	Z	E	P	Z	S	G	B	P
T	J	V	I	B	R	A	T	E	F	O	L
W	J	Q	D	D	W	H	M	A	L	K	X
L	F	J	W	D	E	D	G	P	A	E	W

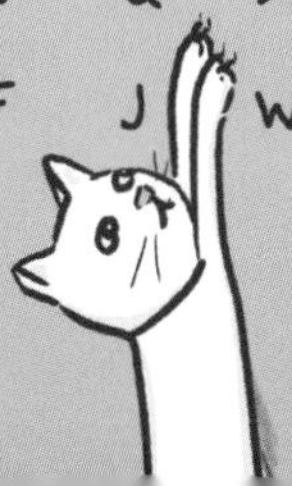

SIMILAR SWEET DISKS

CIRCLE THE TWO PILES OF SWEET DISKS THAT ARE DIFFERENT FROM THE REST.

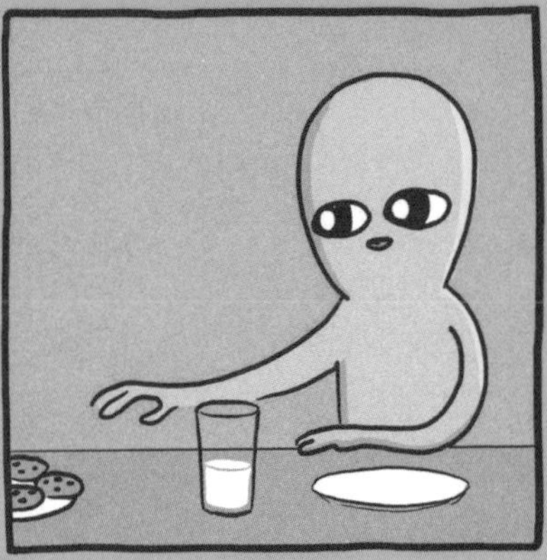

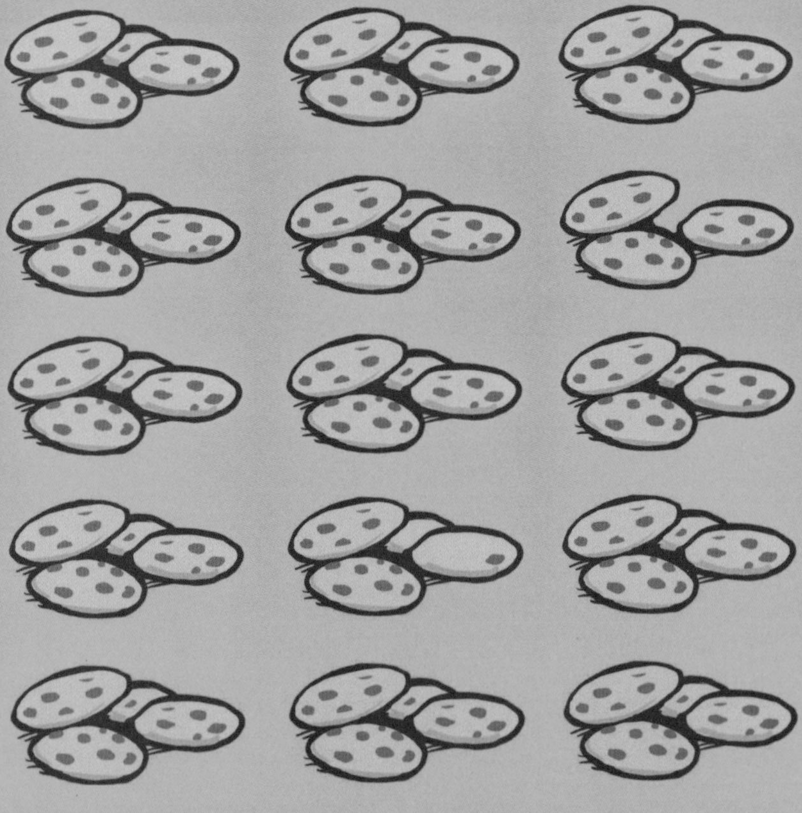

TO FIND THE ANSWER, FILL IN THE LETTERS.

$\overline{12}$ $\overline{9}$ $\quad$ $\overline{5}$ $\overline{8}$ $\overline{4}$ $\overline{9}$ $\quad$ $\overline{6}$ $\overline{3}$ $\overline{8}$ $\overline{1}$

$\overline{9}$ $\overline{7}$ $\overline{8}$ $\overline{12}$ $\overline{1}$ $\quad$ $\overline{7}$ $\overline{8}$ $\overline{11}$ $\overline{2}$

I=12	D=2	T=9	W=5
E=8	R=1	N=4	V=3
O=6	H=7	S=10	A=11

FOOT-ORB CRISS-CROSS PUZZLE

IDENTIFY THE OBJECTS YOU WILL NEED FOR YOUR FOOT-ORB GAME.

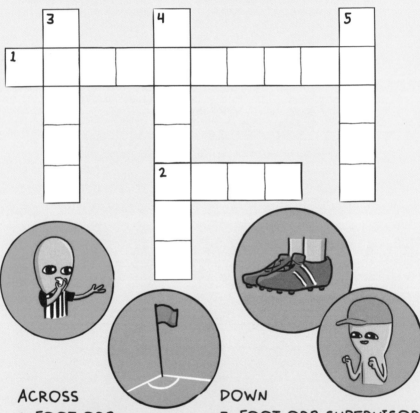

ACROSS
1. FOOT-ORB
2. CRUCIAL REGULATION

DOWN
3. FOOT-ORB SUPERVISOR
4. SHOVE-TIME ARBITER
5. FEET FRICTION

CRUCIAL REGULATION CONFUSION

FIGURE OUT THE ORB TEAM CHEER BY UNSCRAMBLING THE LETTERS.

WHAT IS THE CRUCIAL REGULATION?
NO HANDS ON ORB
WHAT IF THE ORB APPROACHES OUR FACE?
LET THE ORB SMACK YOUR FACE
LET US PUT HANDS TOGETHER
1...2..3
____ ___
______!

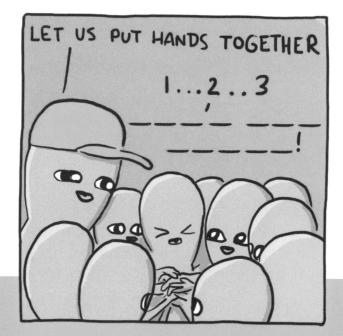

ANCT SEU SHEET

PASS THE ORB

PASS THE ORB TO YOUR MATCHING TEAMMATE
BY DRAWING LINES TO COMPLETE PASSES
A, B, AND C WITHOUT THE LINES CROSSING.

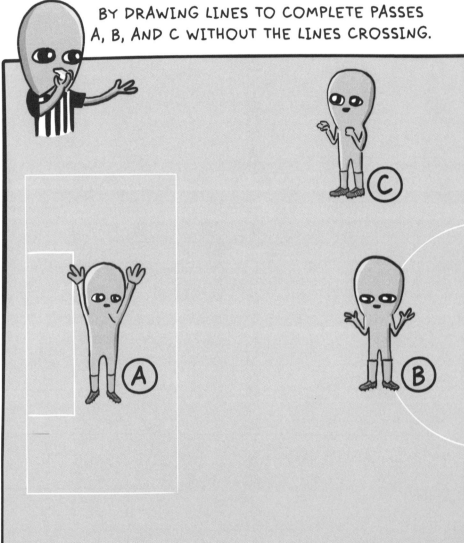

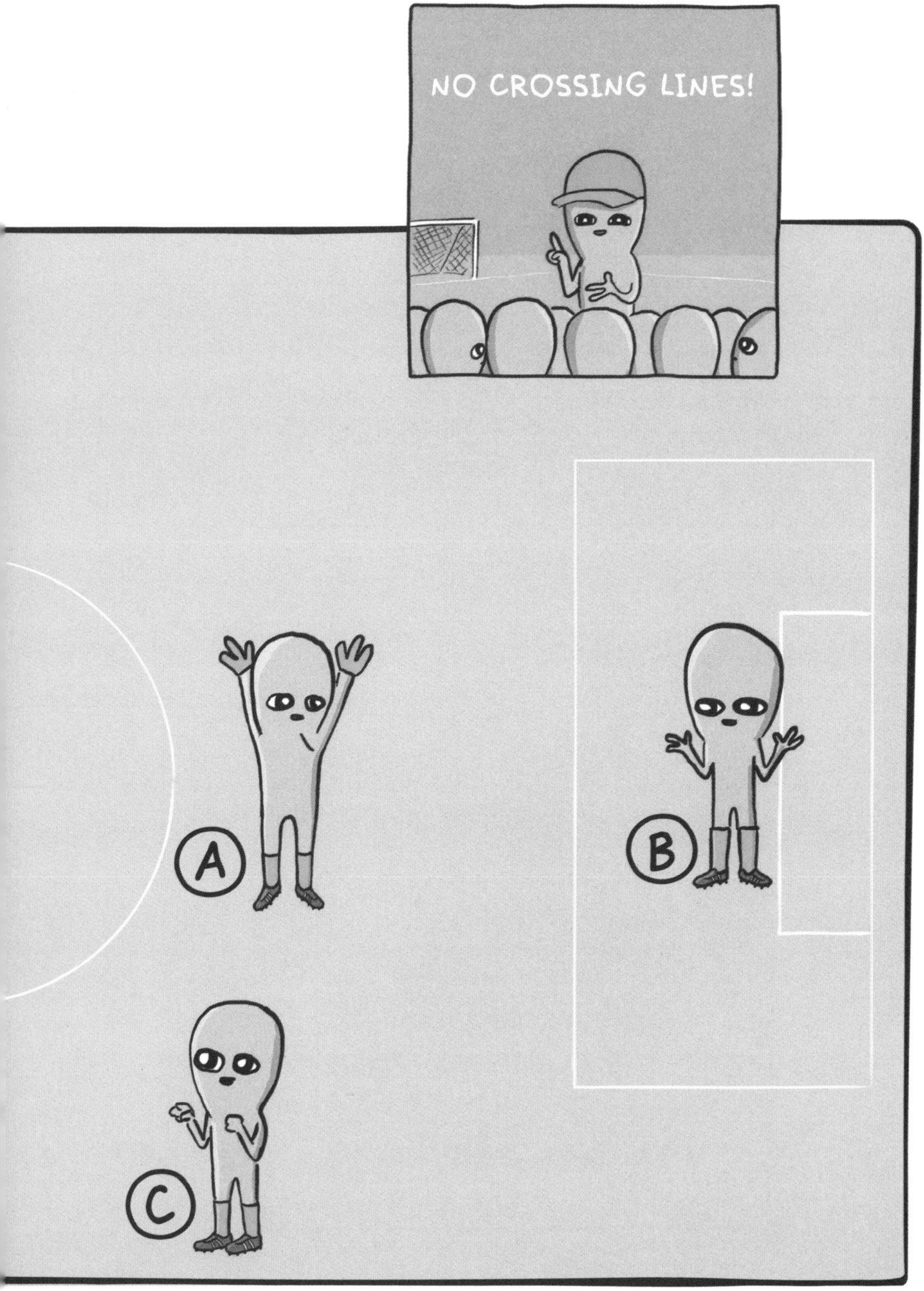
NO CROSSING LINES!
A
B
C

HIGH FRUCTOSE INGESTION

WHY DOES YOUR FOOT-ORB SUPERVISOR GIVE YOU SLICES OF FRUIT? WRITE A LIST OF 4 OTHER ORANGE FOODS THEY CAN GIVE YOU INSTEAD:

______________________ ______________________

______________________ ______________________

NOW INGEST THE TRADITIONAL FRUCTOSE

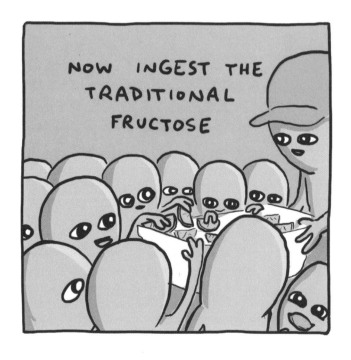

VAST DOUGH CIRCLE

FIND THE TWO VAST DOUGH CIRCLES THAT ARE DIFFERENT FROM THE REST.

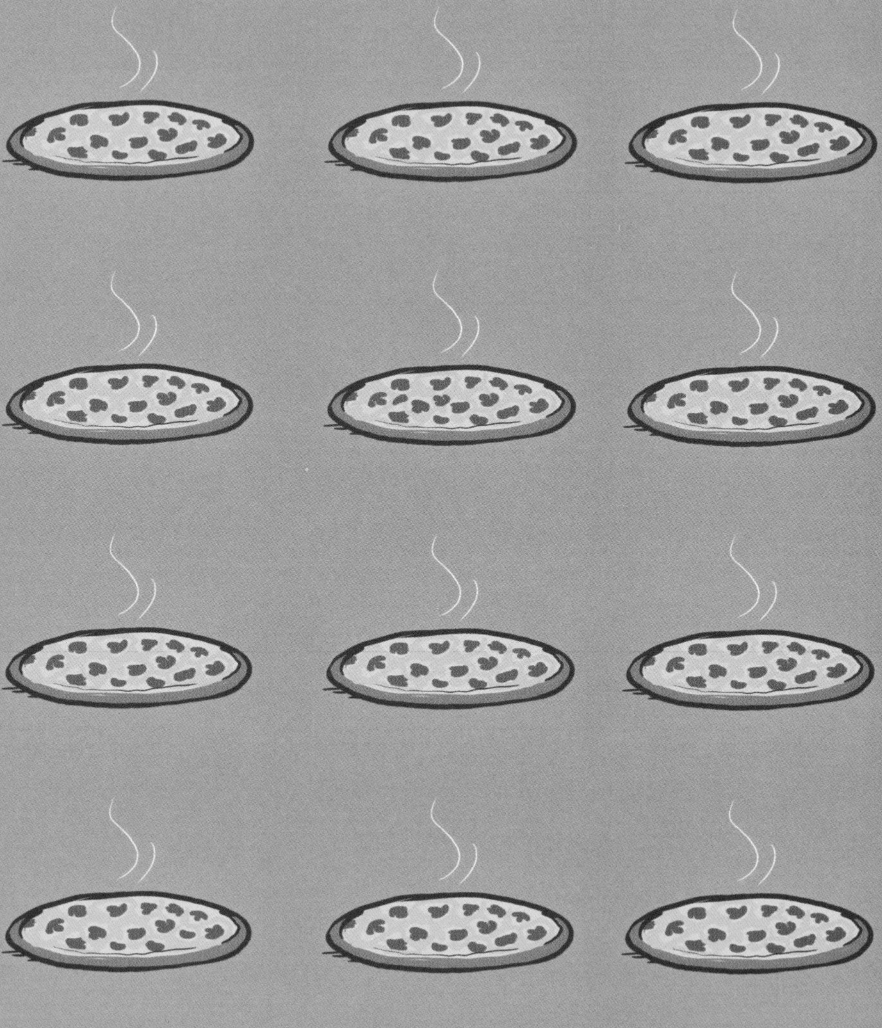

SUSTENANCE DELIVERY OBSERVE THE DISTINCTION

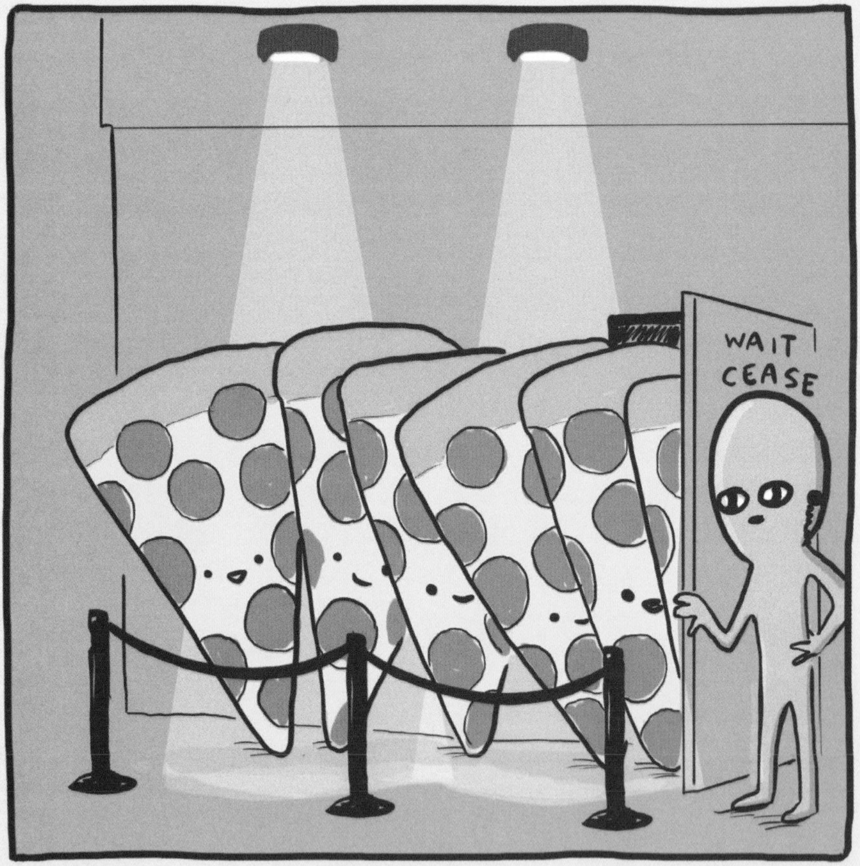
WAIT
CEASE

CIRCLE THE 5 DIFFERENCES BETWEEN THE 2 SCENES.

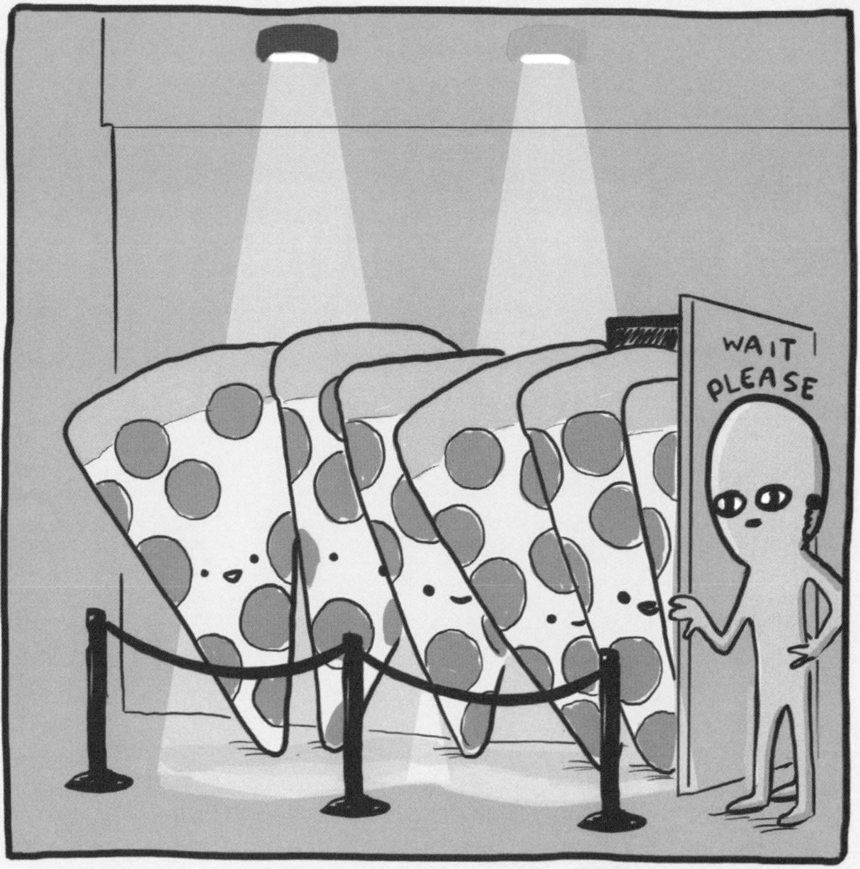
WAIT PLEASE

GROUP-SOFT-SEAT COMFORT SQUARE SUBTRACTION

ANSWER THE MATH PROBLEMS TO SEE THE IDEAL NUMBER OF COMFORT SQUARES NEEDED ON YOUR GROUP-SOFT-SEAT.

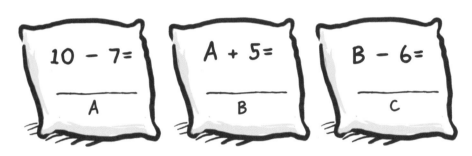

$$10 - 7 = \underline{\hspace{2cm}} \quad A$$

$$A + 5 = \underline{\hspace{2cm}} \quad B$$

$$B - 6 = \underline{\hspace{2cm}} \quad C$$

C IS THE CORRECT NUMBER OF COMFORT SQUARES.

WHAT SAYING WOULD YOU WANT ON YOUR NOVELTY COMFORT SQUARE? WRITE IT IN BELOW.

SURVIVE

CHUCKLE

SHOW AFFECTION

WHAT HAPPENS NEXT?

IN THE LAST TWO PANELS, WRITE WHAT HAPPENS NEXT IN THE SCARY MOVIE AND CREATE A LOW-DETAIL RENDERING OF HOW THE BEINGS REACT.

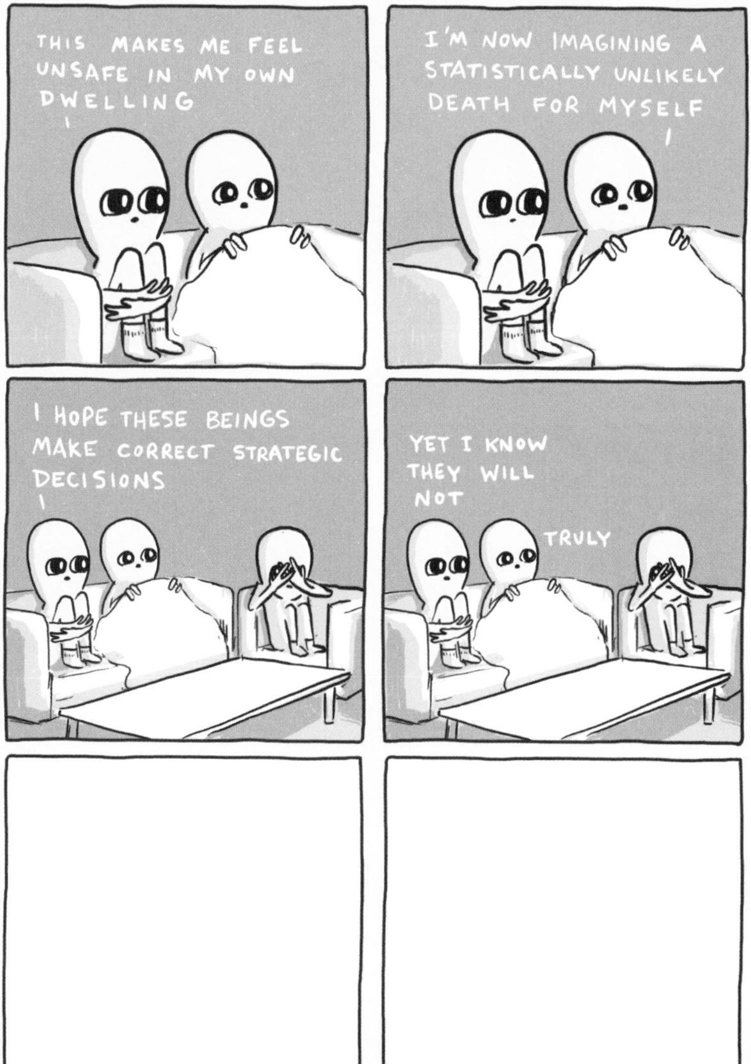

THIS MAKES ME FEEL UNSAFE IN MY OWN DWELLING
I'M NOW IMAGINING A STATISTICALLY UNLIKELY DEATH FOR MYSELF
I HOPE THESE BEINGS MAKE CORRECT STRATEGIC DECISIONS
YET I KNOW THEY WILL NOT
TRULY

EXPLODING GRAINS

SOLVE THE PROBLEM ON EACH PIECE
OF EXPLODED GRAIN TO RECEIVE DOUBLE
FLAVOR AUGMENTATION.

11 + 18=
_____

6 + 13=
_____

10 + 9=
_____

15 + 19=
_____

4 + 14=
_____

ERRATIC CREATURE RESTS

CIRCLE THE WORDS TO DESCRIBE HOW YOU FEEL WITH A CREATURE ON YOUR LAP.

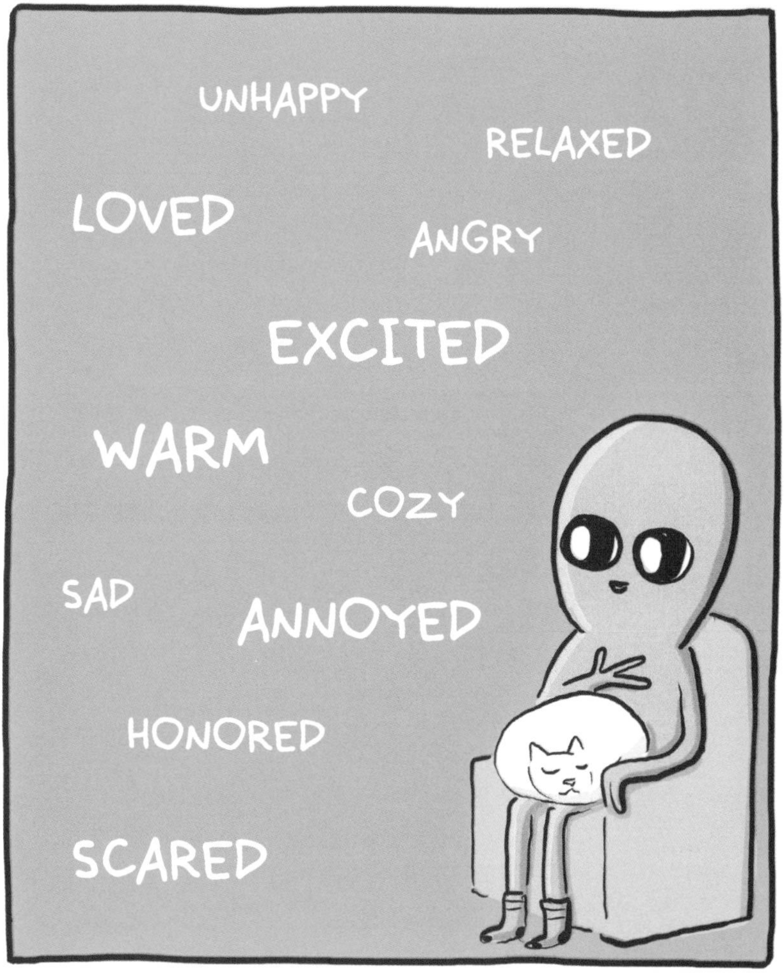
UNHAPPY
RELAXED
LOVED
ANGRY
EXCITED
WARM
COZY
SAD
ANNOYED
HONORED
SCARED

CREATURE FEATURES

LIST THE WORDS FROM THE WORD BANK
UNDER THE CREATURE THEY DESCRIBE.

_____   _____

_____   _____

_____   _____

_____   _____

_____   _____

_____   _____

WORD BANK

FLEXIBLE	YELLS	BEST FRIEND
ERRATIC	LOVES HANDPATS	SNEAKY
VIBRATING	PARADOXICAL	ALOOF
HIGHLY EFFICIENT	SHEDS	AFFECTIONATE

RETIRE TO
REST SLAB CHAMBER

FILL IN THE LETTERS TO DEFINE
THE STRANGE PLANET WORDS.

REST SLAB CHAMBER

_ _ D _ _ _ _

FABRIC CREATURE

_ T _ _ _ _ _ A _ _ _ _ _

REST SLAB

_ E _

STARBLOCK FABRICS

C _ _ _ _ _ _ _

LIQUID ON DEMAND

FILL IN THE BLANKS WITH WORDS FROM THE
BANK TO MAKE A MELODY THAT RHYMES.

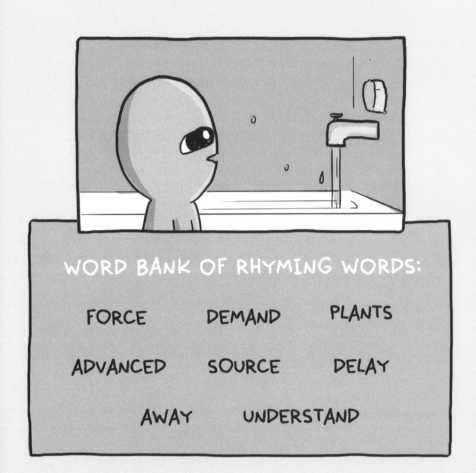

WORD BANK OF RHYMING WORDS:

FORCE   DEMAND   PLANTS

ADVANCED   SOURCE   DELAY

AWAY   UNDERSTAND

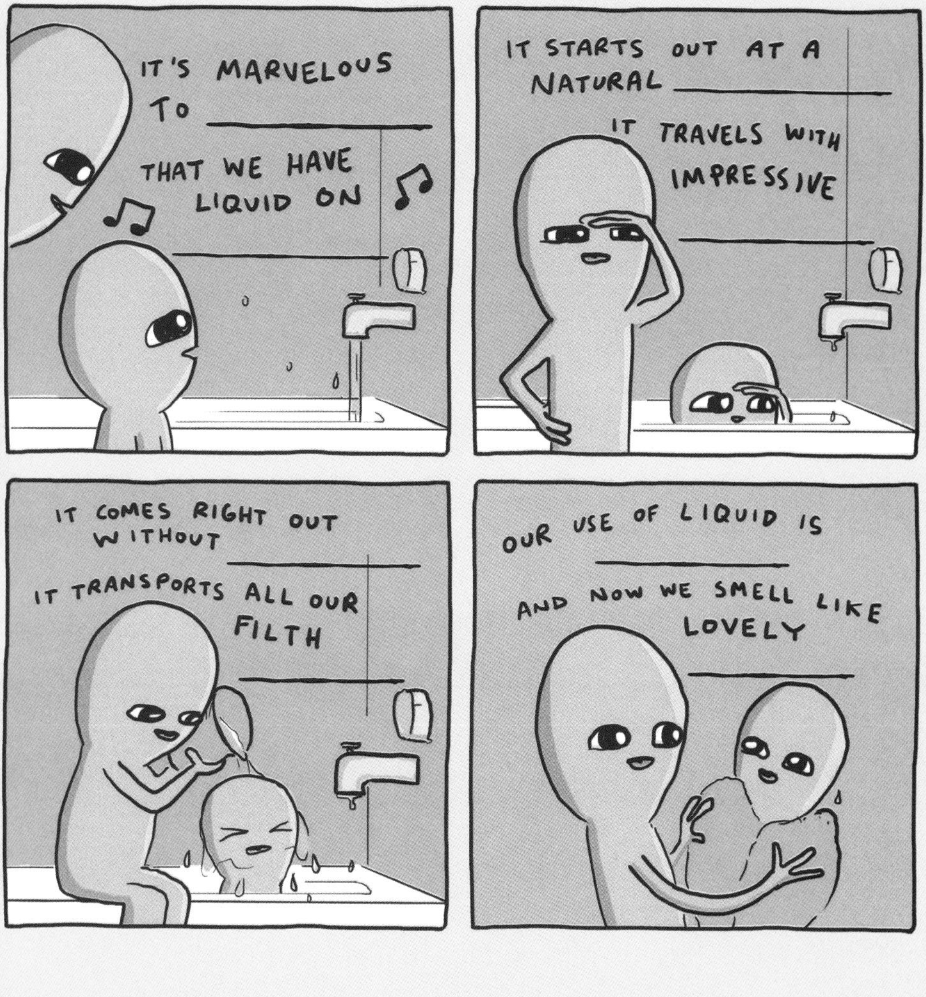

IT'S MARVELOUS TO ________ THAT WE HAVE LIQUID ON ________
IT STARTS OUT AT A NATURAL ________
IT TRAVELS WITH IMPRESSIVE ________
IT COMES RIGHT OUT WITHOUT ________
IT TRANSPORTS ALL OUR FILTH ________
OUR USE OF LIQUID IS ________
AND NOW WE SMELL LIKE LOVELY ________

STARE INTO THE VOID!
THE VOID IS FILLED WITH GASEOUS ORBS! SOME FORM GASEOUS ORB ILLUSTRATIONS. CONNECT THE ODD-NUMBERED DOTS TO SEE ONE!
WHAT WISHES ARE THE BEINGS MAKING? WRITE THEM HERE.

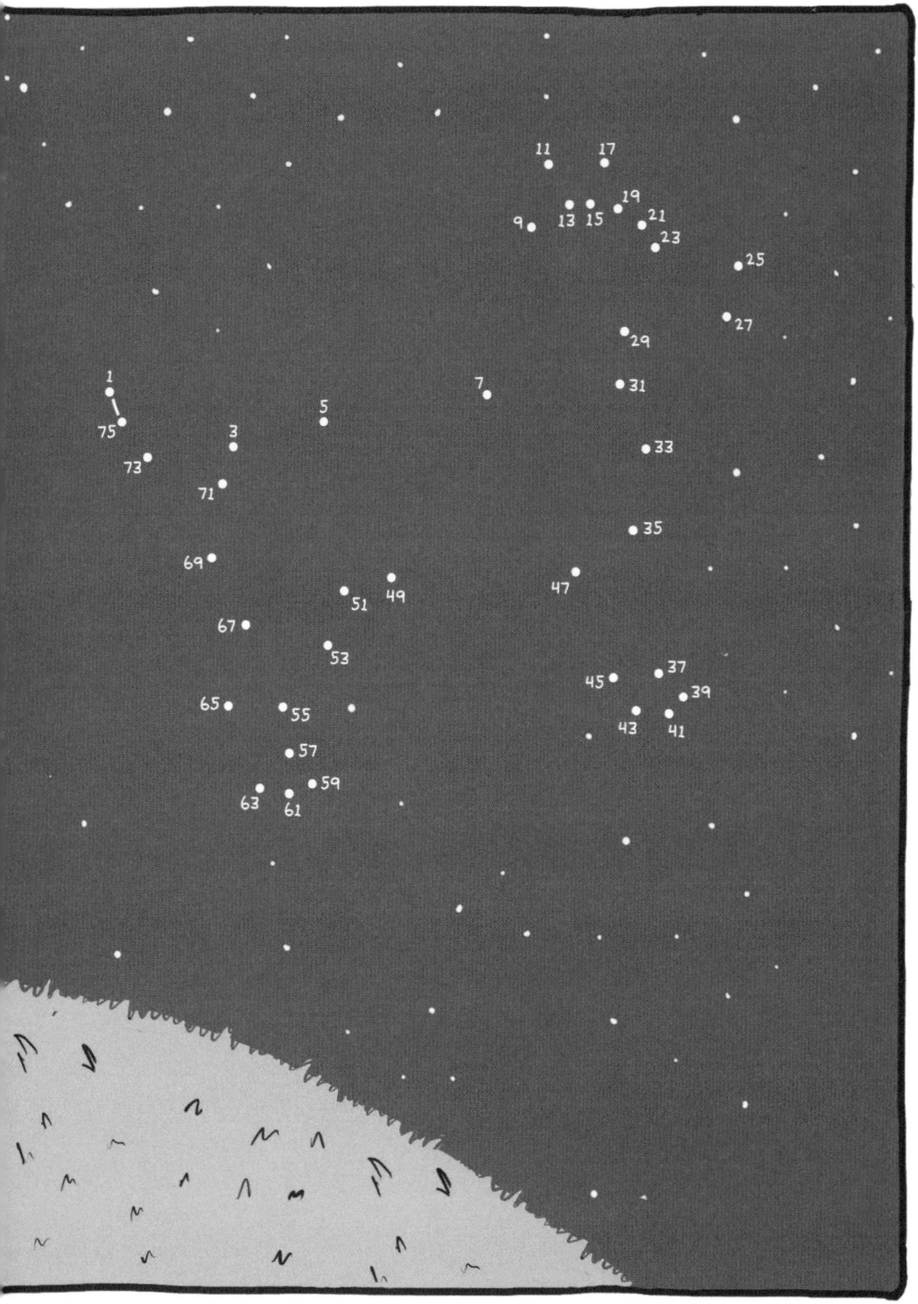
11
17
19
9
13
15
21
23
25
27
29
1
7
31
5
75
3
33
73
71
35
69
47
51
49
67
53
37
45
39
65
55
43
41
57
59
63
61

SEMICONSCIOUS STATE SUDOKU

REACH A SEMICONSCIOUS STATE BY FILLING IN THE EMPTY SQUARES WITH THE NUMBERS AND SHAPES.

HERE'S AN EXAMPLE:

BE SURE TO USE EACH OF THEM JUST ONCE
IN EACH ROW AND IN EACH COLUMN.

ERRATIC CREATURE OBSERVE THE DISTINCTION

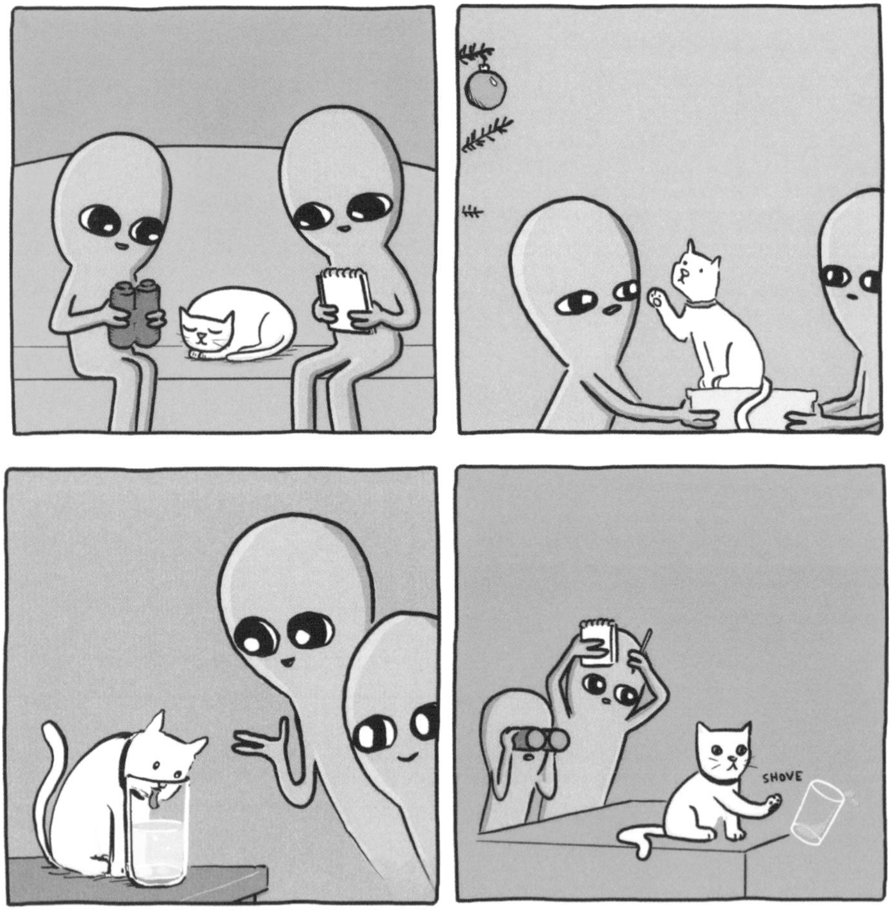
SHOVE

CIRCLE THE DIFFERENCE FOUND IN EACH OF THE 4 SCENES.

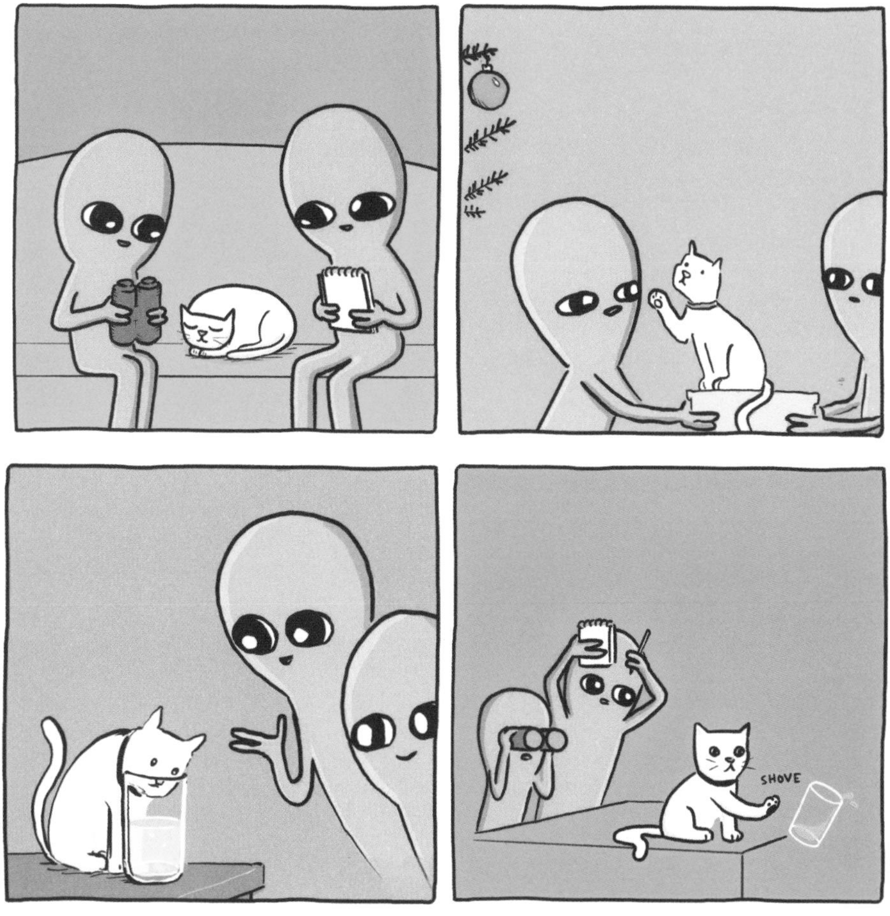
SHOVE

EMERGENCE DAY
THOUGHTFUL DECEPTION

YOU ARE THROWING A
SURPRISE PARTY FOR
A BEING'S EMERGENCE DAY.
CREATE A LOW-DETAIL
RENDERING OF THE CAKE.
↓

ELASTIC BREATH TRAPS
SEEK AND FIND

BEINGS ARE LOST AMONG THE ELASTIC BREATH
TRAPS! CIRCLE THEM WHEN YOU SPOT THEM.

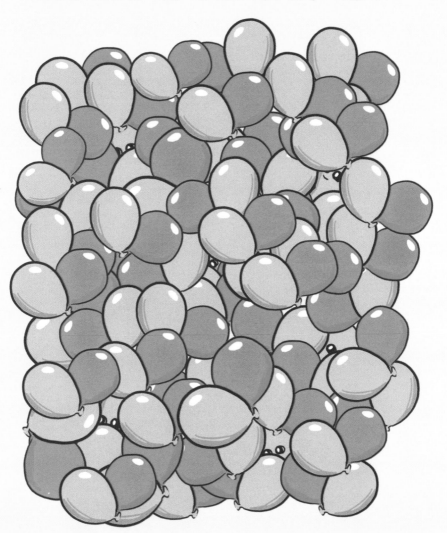

CALCULATE THE SWEET DISKS

COMPLETE THE PROBLEMS. THEN SEARCH FOR THE 3 NUMBERS IN THE PROBLEM IN THE SEARCH ON THE RIGHT.

THE FIRST ONE IS DONE FOR YOU.

2x2= 4

2x3= ______

2x4= ______

2x5= ______

2x6= ______

2x7= ______

2x8= ______

2x9= ______

2x10= ______

2x11= ______

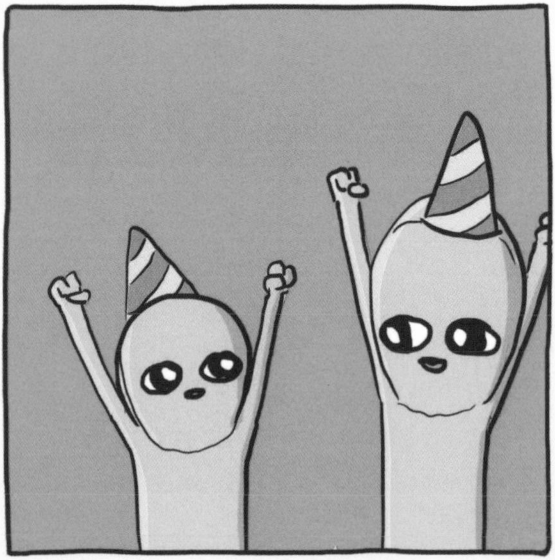

2   4   8   5   6   10   7   9   2   2

8   12   4   7   2   9   6   3   5   8

3   5   2   12   24   2   6   8   6   16

18   2   12   8   6   15   22   3   9   1

22   11   2   6   12   2   5   4   12   16

4   8   19   20   1   9   18   7   11   2

9   24   8   3   7   12   10   6   2   16

16   8   14   7   2   9   22   4   5   20

3   9   2   18   8   10   5   2   18   14

8   12   4   5   6   8   20   9   2   7

THOUGHTFUL DECEPTION GAME

FLIP A CURRENCY DISK TO TRAVEL FROM TURNING OFF THE LIGHTS TO THE MOMENT OF THOUGHTFUL DECEPTION.

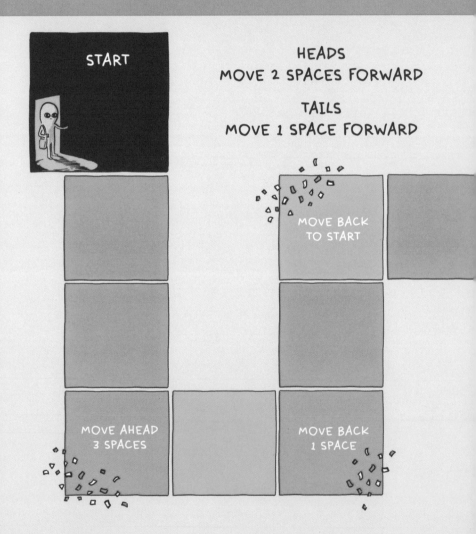

START

HEADS
MOVE 2 SPACES FORWARD

TAILS
MOVE 1 SPACE FORWARD

MOVE BACK
TO START

MOVE AHEAD
3 SPACES

MOVE BACK
1 SPACE

FOLLOW THE INSTRUCTIONS ON THE SPACE WHERE YOU LAND.
IF IT'S BLANK, FLIP THE COIN AGAIN.
TRY TO REACH THE THOUGHTFUL DECEPTION IN AS FEW COIN FLIPS AS POSSIBLE.

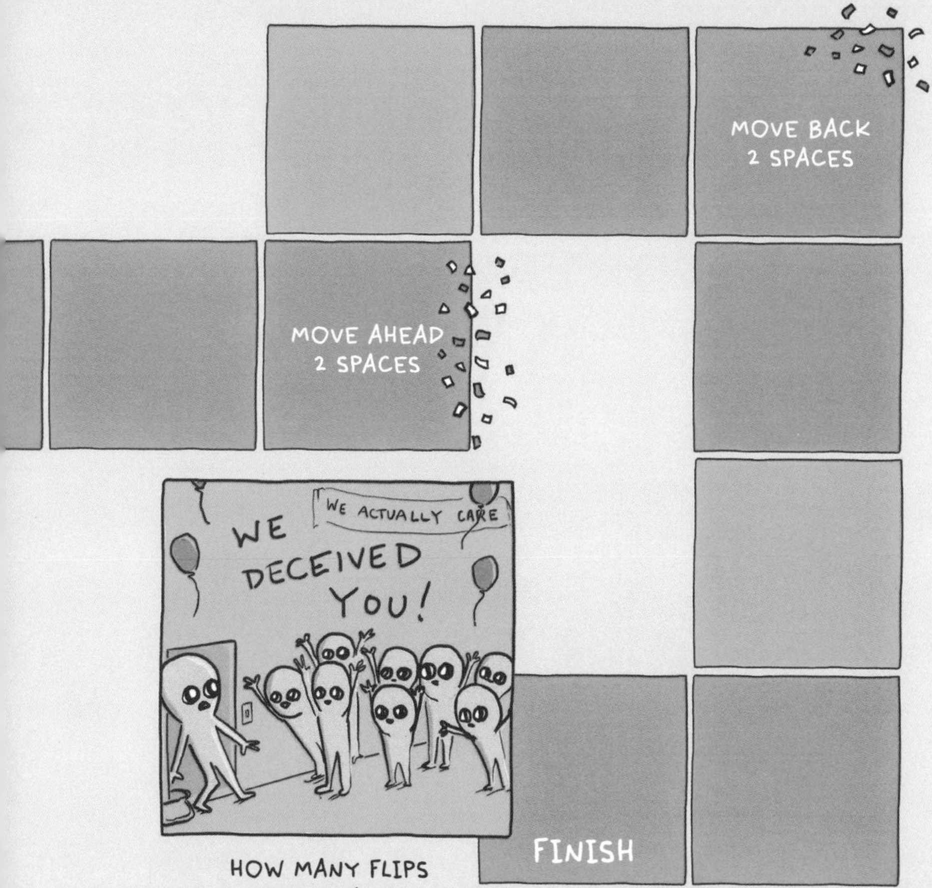

MOVE BACK 2 SPACES
MOVE AHEAD 2 SPACES
WE ACTUALLY CARE
WE DECEIVED YOU!
FINISH

HOW MANY FLIPS DID IT TAKE?

____

CONCEALMENT DESTRUCTION

CROSS OUT THE CONCEALED SURPRISES YOU WOULD NOT LIKE TO RECEIVE.

SURVIVE
CHUCKLE
SHOW AFFECTION
LEAF SMELL

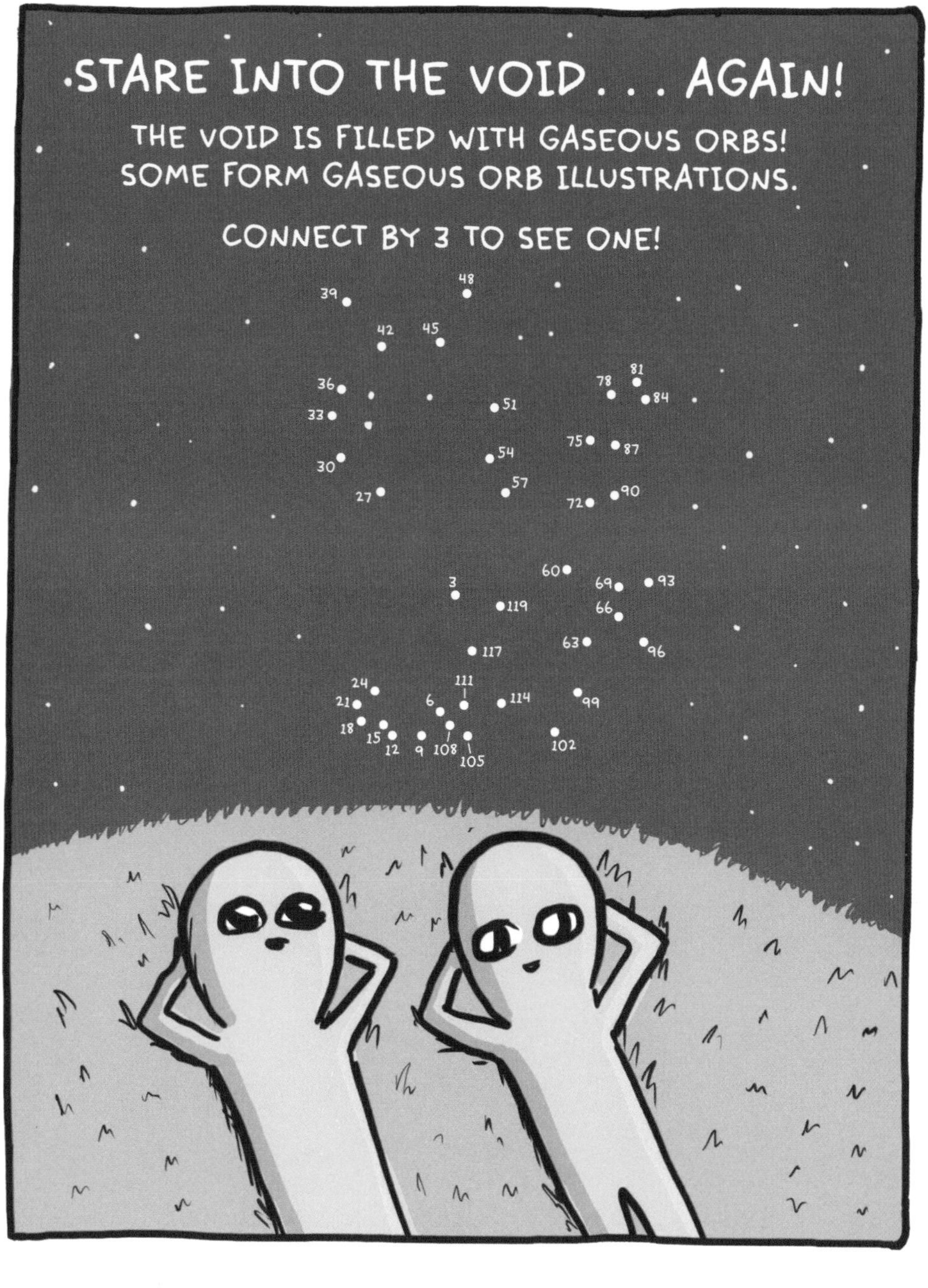

STARE INTO THE VOID. . . AGAIN!
THE VOID IS FILLED WITH GASEOUS ORBS! SOME FORM GASEOUS ORB ILLUSTRATIONS.
CONNECT BY 3 TO SEE ONE!

CREATE 10 WORDS USING LETTERS FROM THE PHRASE "HAPPY EMERGENCE DAY!"

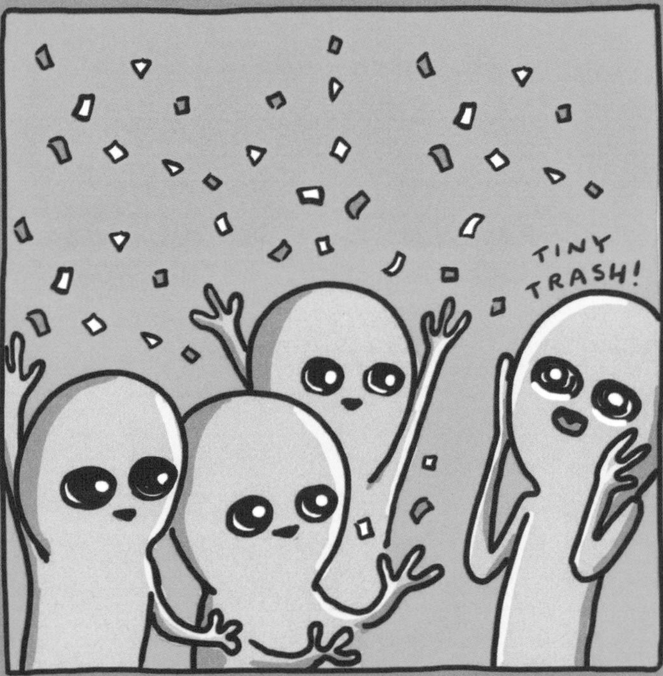
TINY TRASH!

HAPPY EMERGENCE DAY!

THE FIRST ONE IS
DONE FOR YOU!

1 CANDY _____

2 _____

3 _____

4 _____

5 _____

6 _____

7 _____

8 _____

9 _____

10 _____

STAR DAMAGE
CRISS-CROSS PUZZLE

DON'T GET STAR DAMAGE WHILE
FIGURING OUT THIS CROSSWORD.

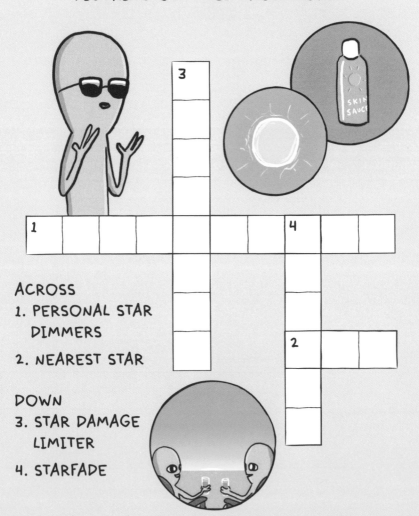

ACROSS
1. PERSONAL STAR
   DIMMERS
2. NEAREST STAR

DOWN
3. STAR DAMAGE
   LIMITER
4. STARFADE

RECREATIONAL BATHING

FINISH THE STORY BY FILLING IN THE TEXT FOR THE LAST PANEL.

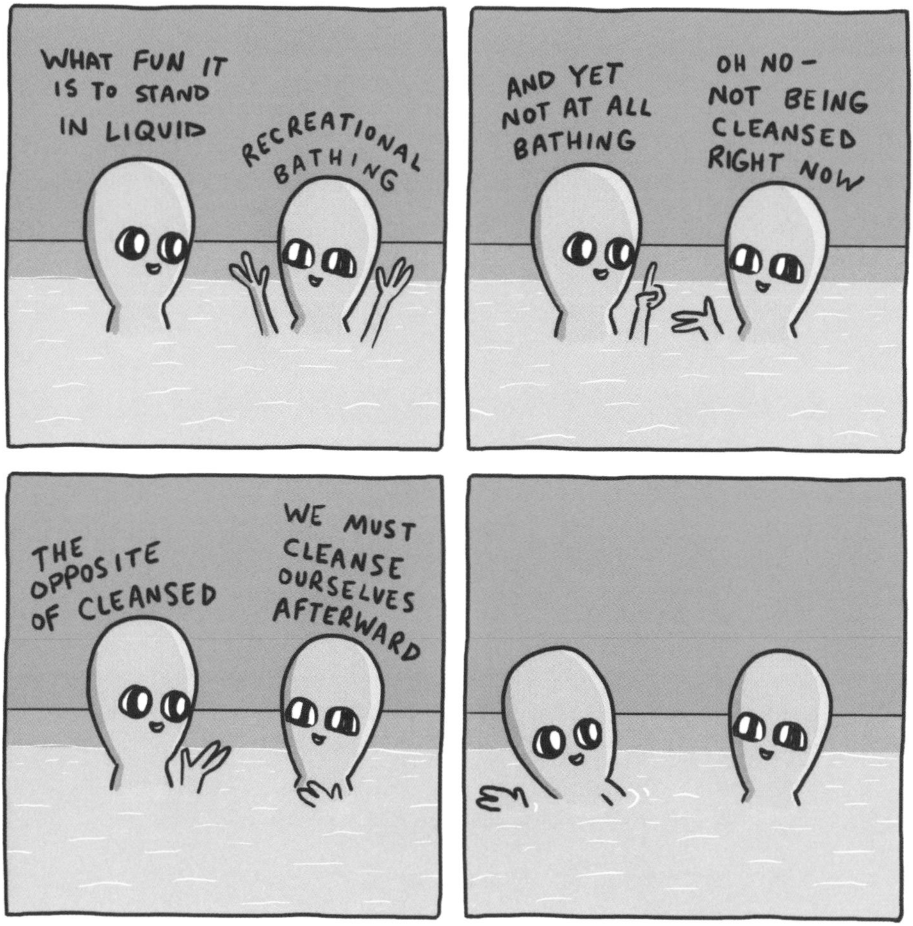
WHAT FUN IT IS TO STAND IN LIQUID
RECREATIONAL BATHING
AND YET NOT AT ALL BATHING
OH NO - NOT BEING CLEANSED RIGHT NOW
THE OPPOSITE OF CLEANSED
WE MUST CLEANSE OURSELVES AFTERWARD

EPHEMERAL SPHERES

DRAW STRAIGHT LINES TO CONNECT SPHERES THAT ADD UP TO 35. USE ONLY THREE BUBBLES EACH TIME. LINES MUST ONLY TOUCH BUBBLES WITH NUMBERS! THERE ARE MULTIPLE ANSWERS.

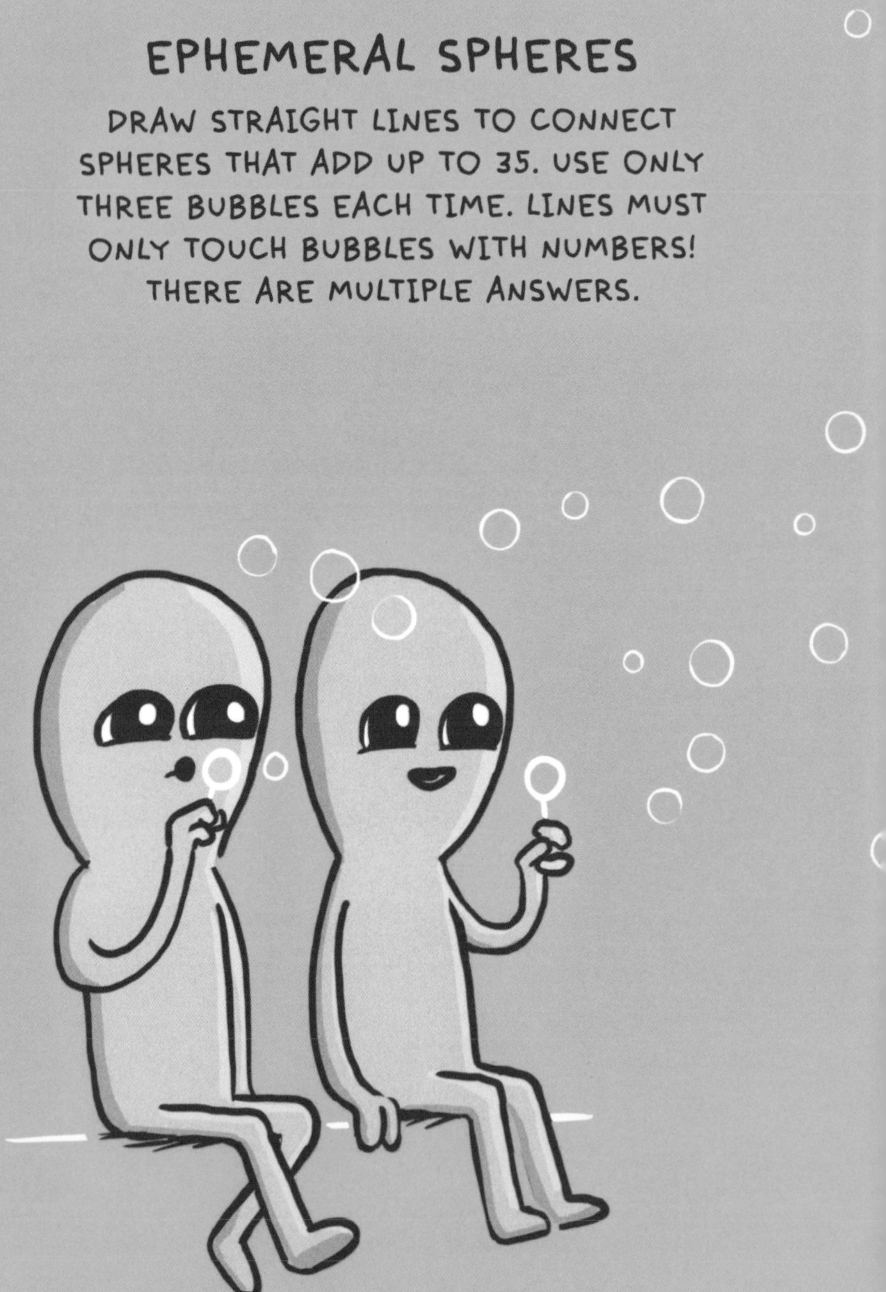

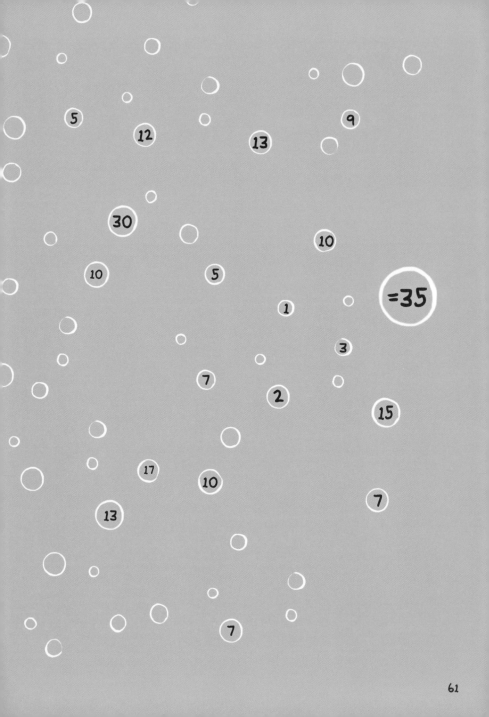

OBSERVE THE ORB-CATCHER SUDOKU

OBSERVE THE ORB-CATCHER BY FILLING IN THE EMPTY SQUARES WITH THE NUMBERS AND ORBS.

HERE'S AN EXAMPLE:

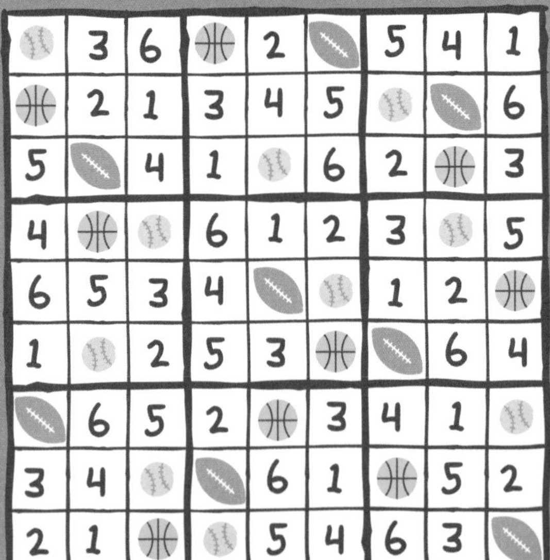

⚾	3	6	🏀	2	🏈	5	4	1
🏀	2	1	3	4	5	⚾	🏈	6
5	🏈	4	1	⚾	6	2	🏀	3
4	🏀	⚾	6	1	2	3	⚾	5
6	5	3	4	🏈	⚾	1	2	🏀
1	⚾	2	5	3	🏀	🏈	6	4
🏈	6	5	2	🏀	3	4	1	⚾
3	4	⚾	🏈	6	1	🏀	5	2
2	1	🏀	⚾	5	4	6	3	🏈

BE SURE TO USE EACH OF THEM JUST ONCE IN EACH ROW AND IN EACH COLUMN.

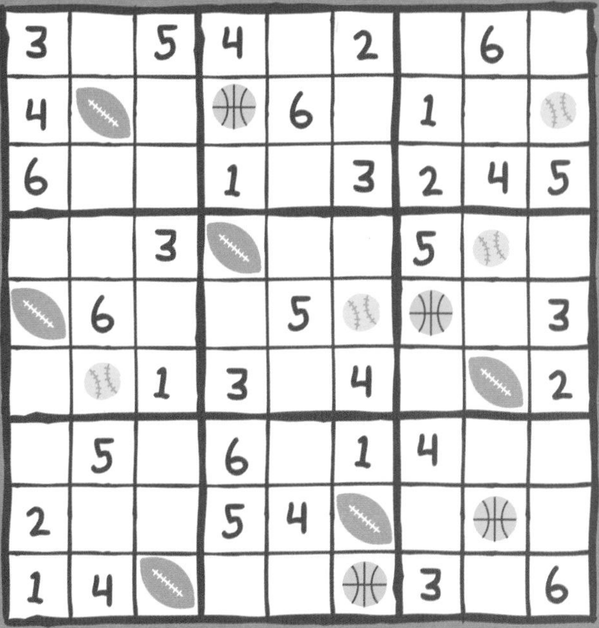

3		5	4		2		6	
4				6		1		
6			1		3	2	4	5
		3				5		
	6			5				3
		1	3		4			2
	5		6		1	4		
2			5	4				
1	4					3		6

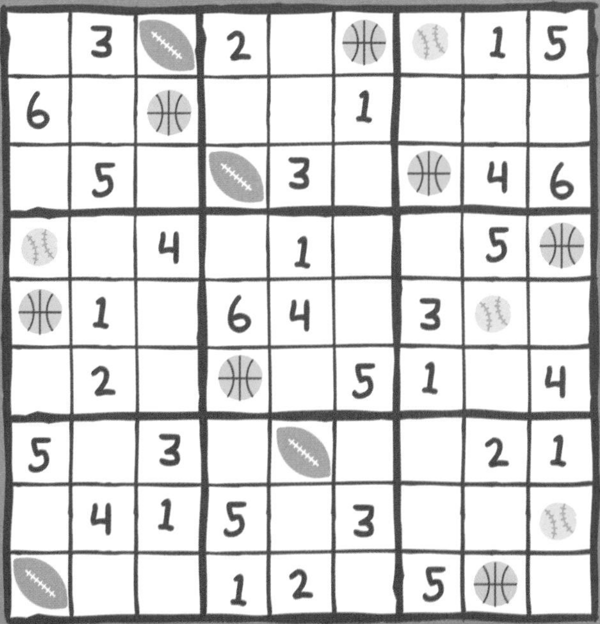

	3		2				1	5
6					1			
	5			3			4	6
		4		1			5	
	1		6	4		3		
	2				5	1		4
5		3					2	1
	4	1	5		3			
			1	2		5		

NEARLY PERISHING FOR FUN CRYPTOGRAM

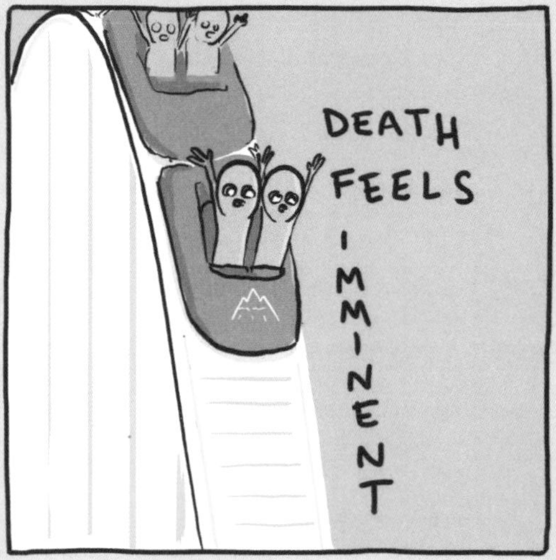
DEATH
FEELS
IMMINENT

R=N	L=D	A=E
O=W	E=T	S=O
	C=I	

WHAT DID THE BEINGS
SAY AFTER NEARLY
PERISHING FOR FUN?

TO FIND THE ANSWER, FILL IN THE LETTERS.

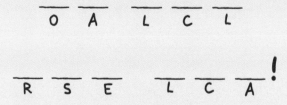

$\overline{}$ $\overline{O}$ $\overline{A}$ $\overline{L}$ $\overline{C}$ $\overline{L}$

$\overline{R}$ $\overline{S}$ $\overline{E}$ $\overline{L}$ $\overline{C}$ $\overline{A}$!

NATURAL BODY OF LIQUID MYSTERY MOVEMENT

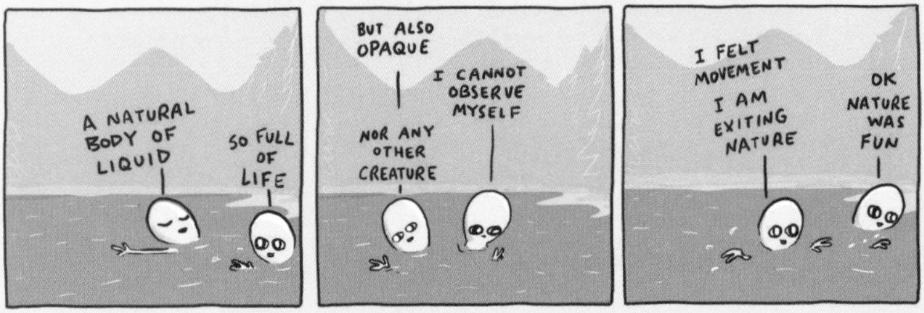

A NATURAL BODY OF LIQUID
SO FULL OF LIFE
BUT ALSO OPAQUE
NOR ANY OTHER CREATURE
I CANNOT OBSERVE MYSELF
I FELT MOVEMENT
I AM EXITING NATURE
OK NATURE WAS FUN

CREATE A LOW-DENSITY RENDERING OF WHAT CREATURES LIVE IN THE NATURAL BODY OF LIQUID

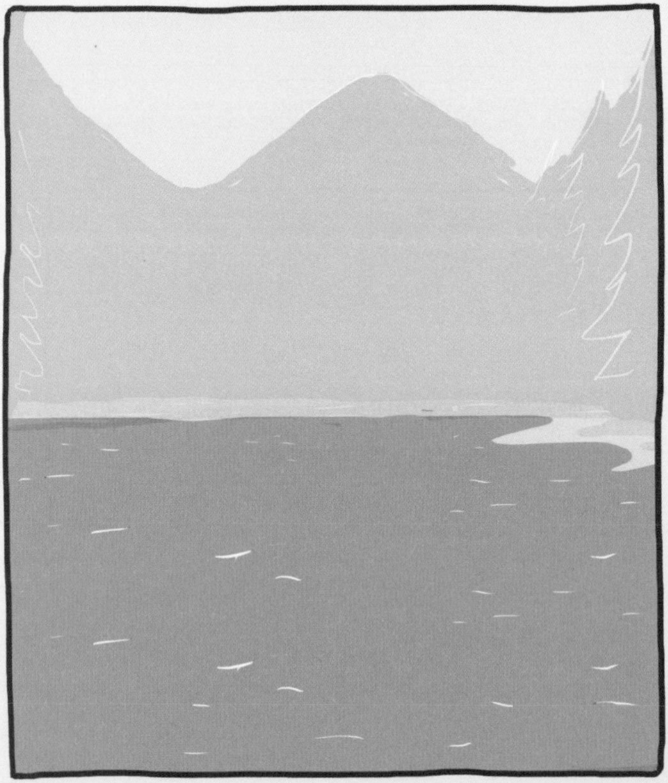

FLYING CREATURE WORD FLIGHT

REPLACE ONE LETTER EACH TIME
TO GET FROM START TO FINISH.

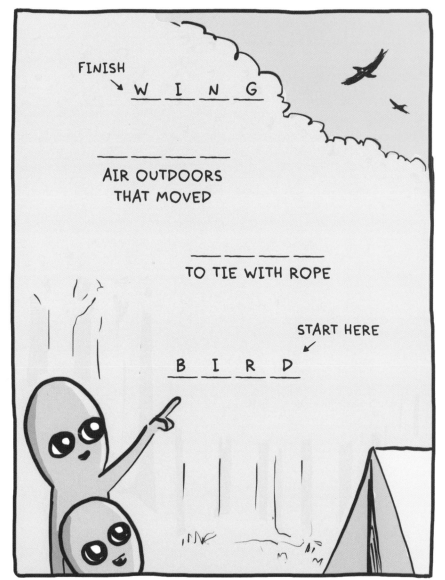

FINISH

W I N G

_ _ _ _

AIR OUTDOORS
THAT MOVED

_ _ _ _

TO TIE WITH ROPE

START HERE

B I R D

PERISHED LEAVES PILE SEARCH

CAN YOU FIND THE THREE CREATURES HIDING IN THE PERISHED LEAVES?

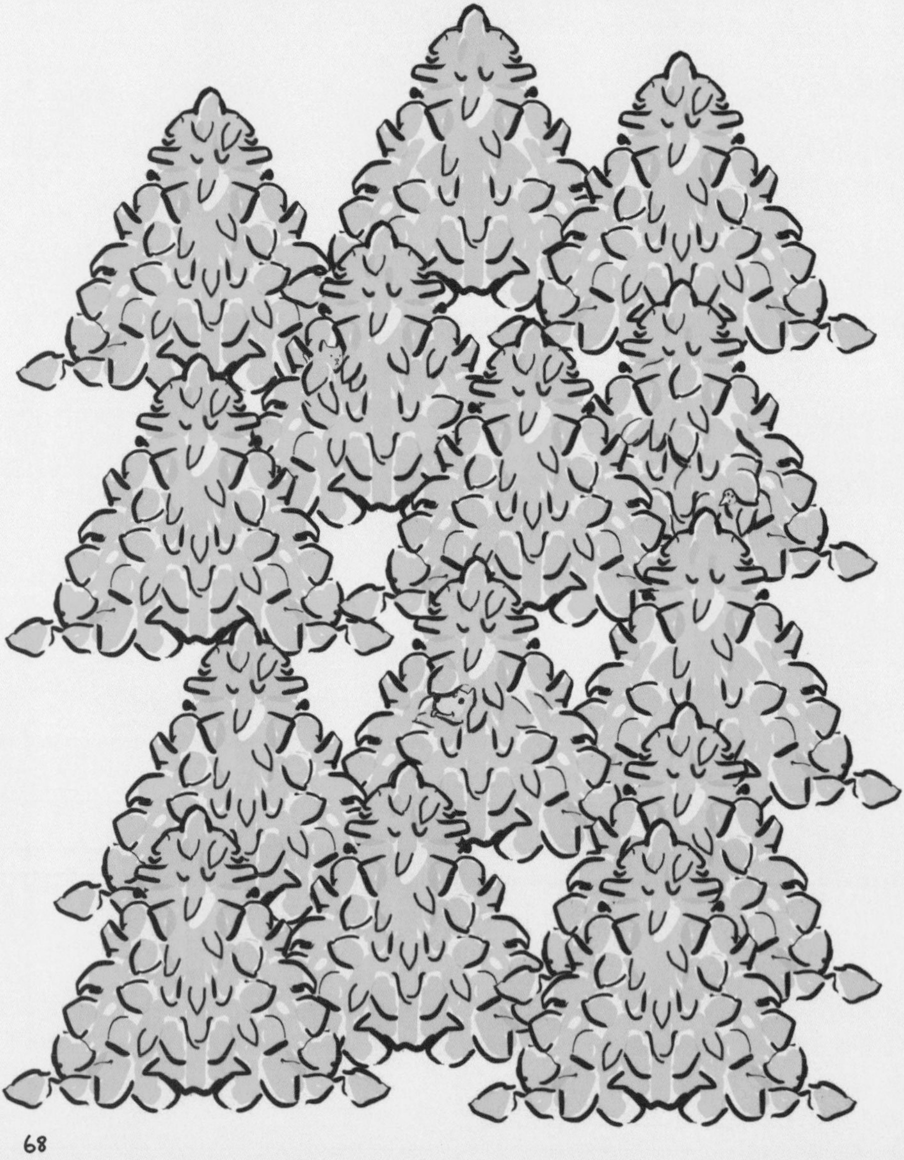

HOW DO YOU FEEL TODAY?

DRAW THE FEATURES ON A BEING
THAT SHOW HOW YOU FEEL.

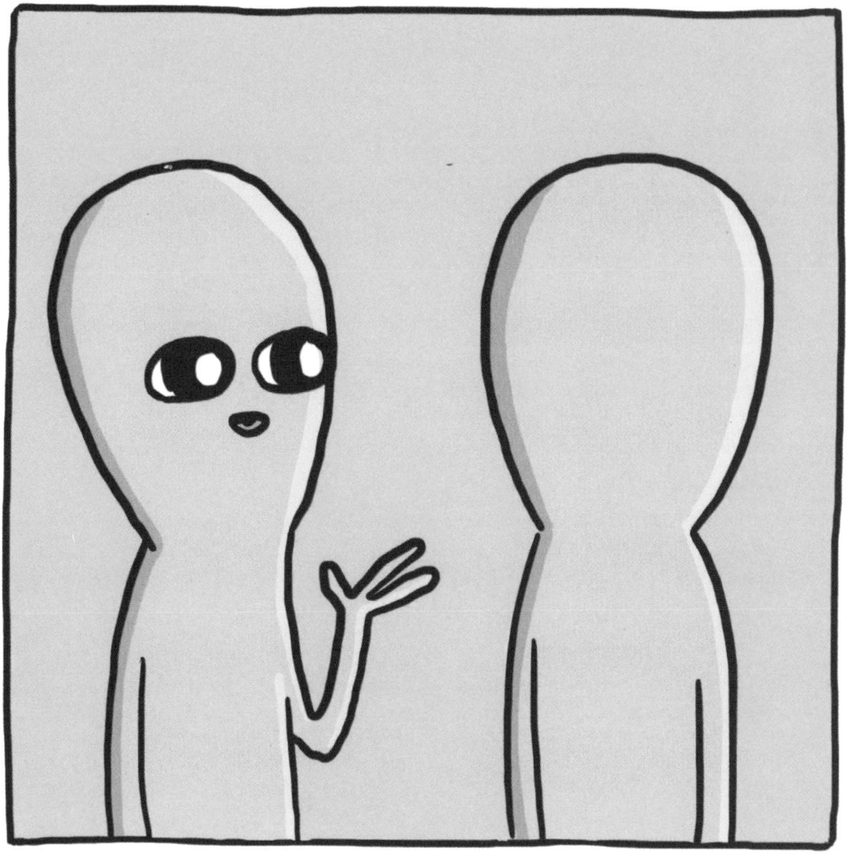

OBSERVE THE DISTINCTION

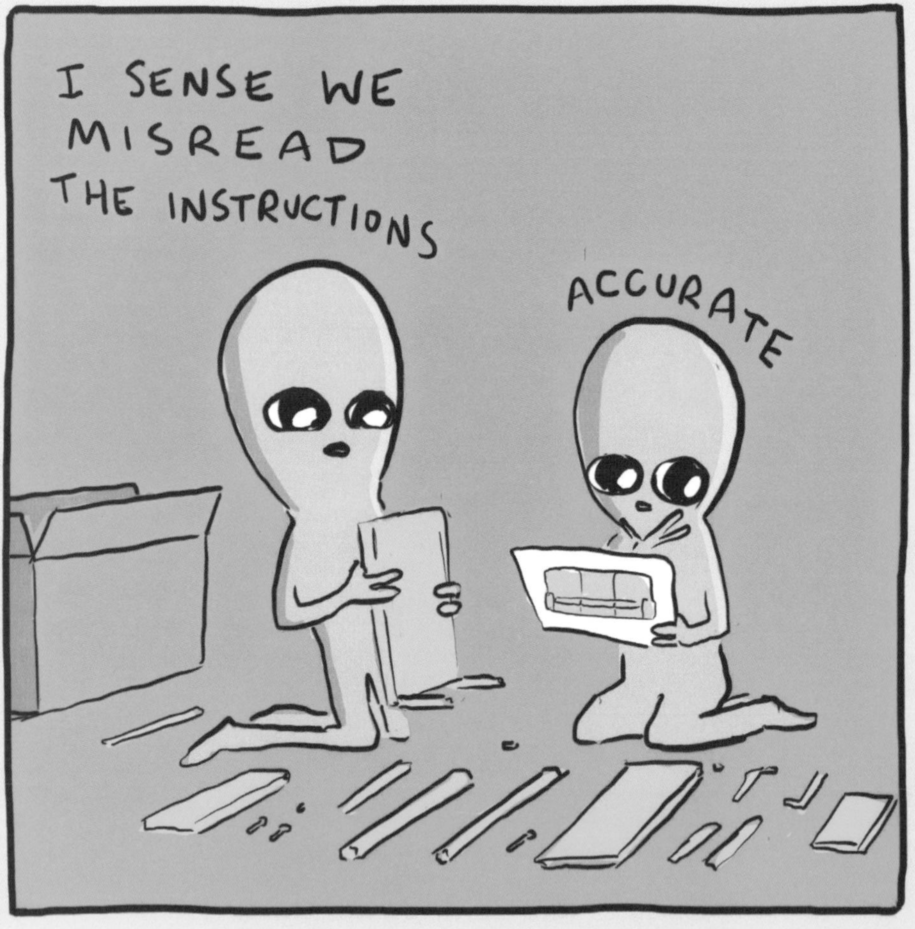

I SENSE WE MISREAD THE INSTRUCTIONS
ACCURATE

CIRCLE THE 5 DIFFERENCES BETWEEN THE 2 SCENES.

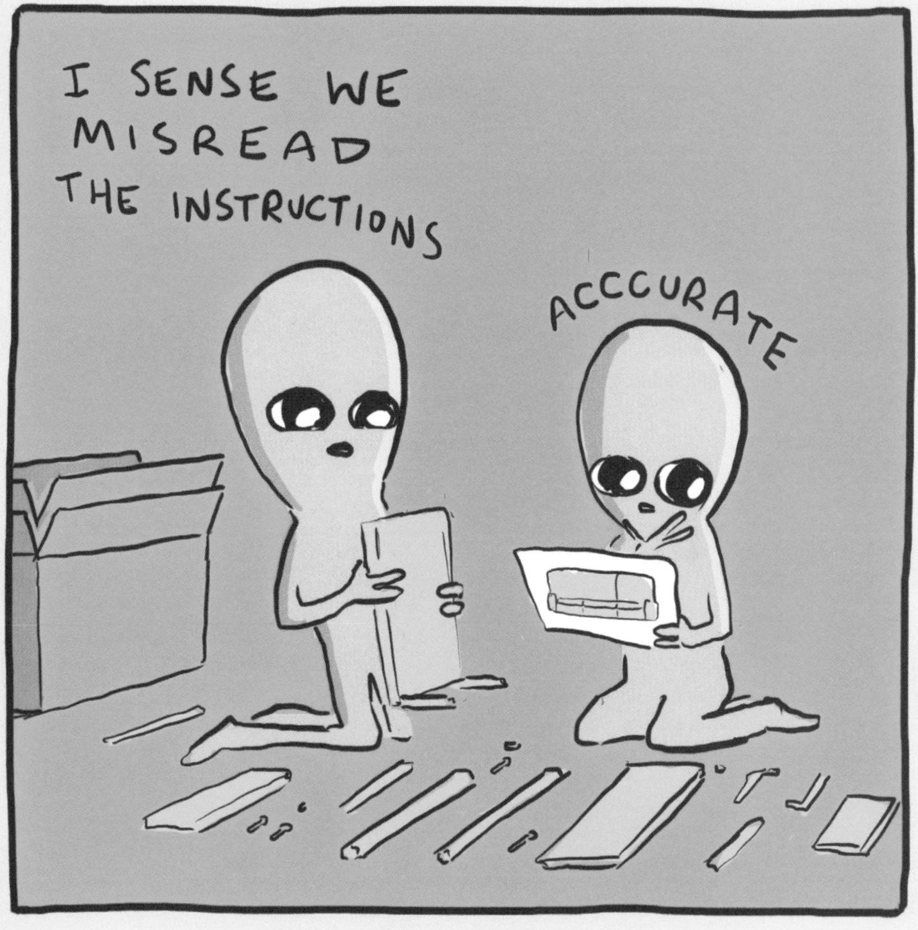
I SENSE WE MISREAD THE INSTRUCTIONS
ACCCURATE

OBSCURE-AND-PURSUE
WORD MATCH

DRAW A LINE BETWEEN THE PHRASE
AND WHAT IT MEANS.

OBSCURE-AND-PURSUE	HERE I COME
I AM APPROACHING	READY OR NOT
RESTRICTING MY VISION	HIDE-AND-SEEK
PREPARED OR NOT	COVER MY EYES

WHAT'S THE NAME OF THE GAME THE BEINGS ARE PLAYING?

_____

WHERE ARE YOUR FAVORITE SECRET HIDING SPOTS?

_____

_____

_____

_____

ODD BEING OUT

CROSS OUT ALL BEINGS THAT:
- HAVE ORB CATCHER HATS ON
- ARE NOT SMILING
- HAVE AUDITORY MELODYBLASTERS

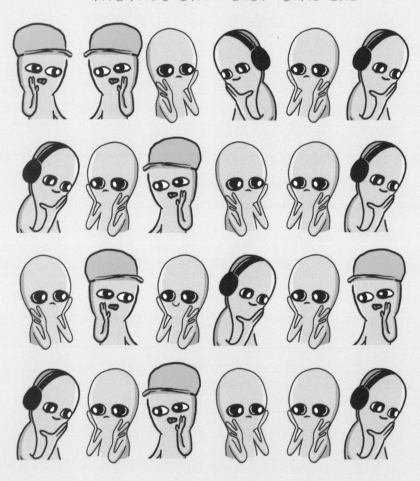

MATCH THE OBJECTS IN YOUR HOME TO WHAT THEY ARE CALLED.

SPINBLASTER

HOT DANGER
SCREAMER

ROLLSUCK

SUSTENANCE
PRESERVER

HEATBLASTER

STARLIGHT
ACCESS PANEL

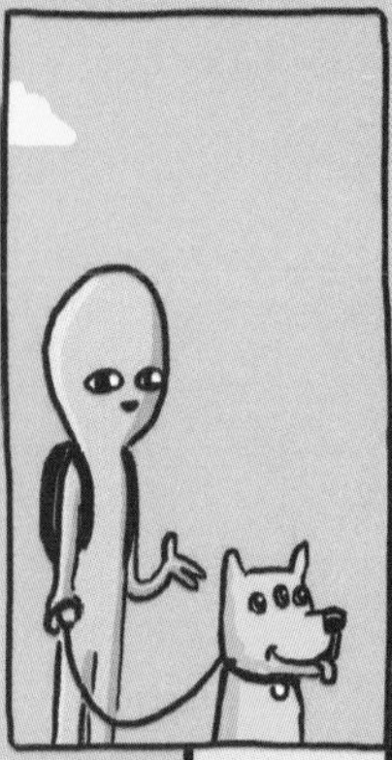

CREATURE WALK MAZE

LEAD THE MORAL CREATURE THROUGH THE MAZE TO HANDPATS.

START →

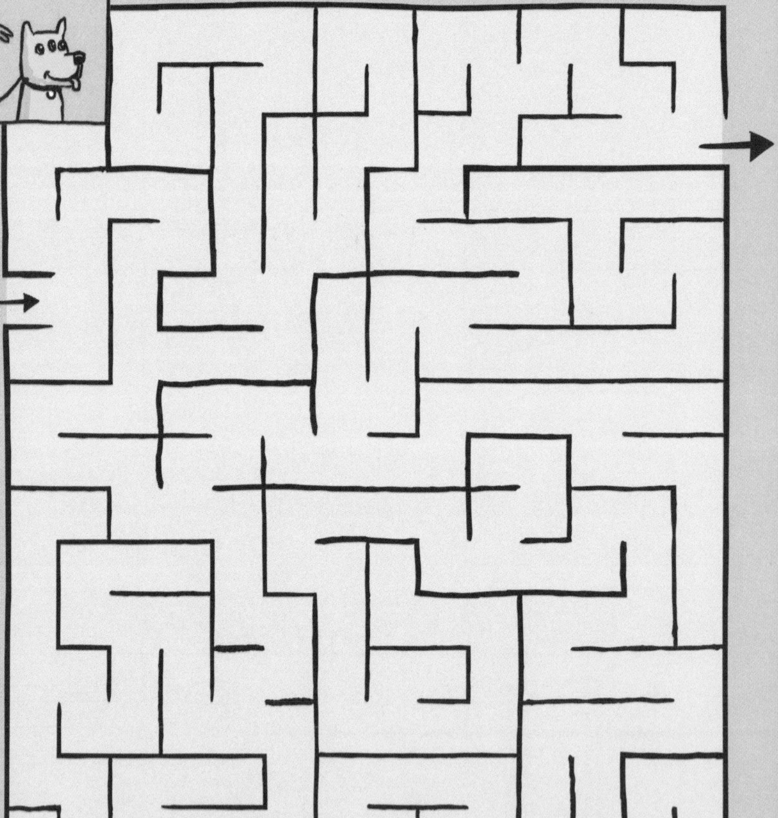

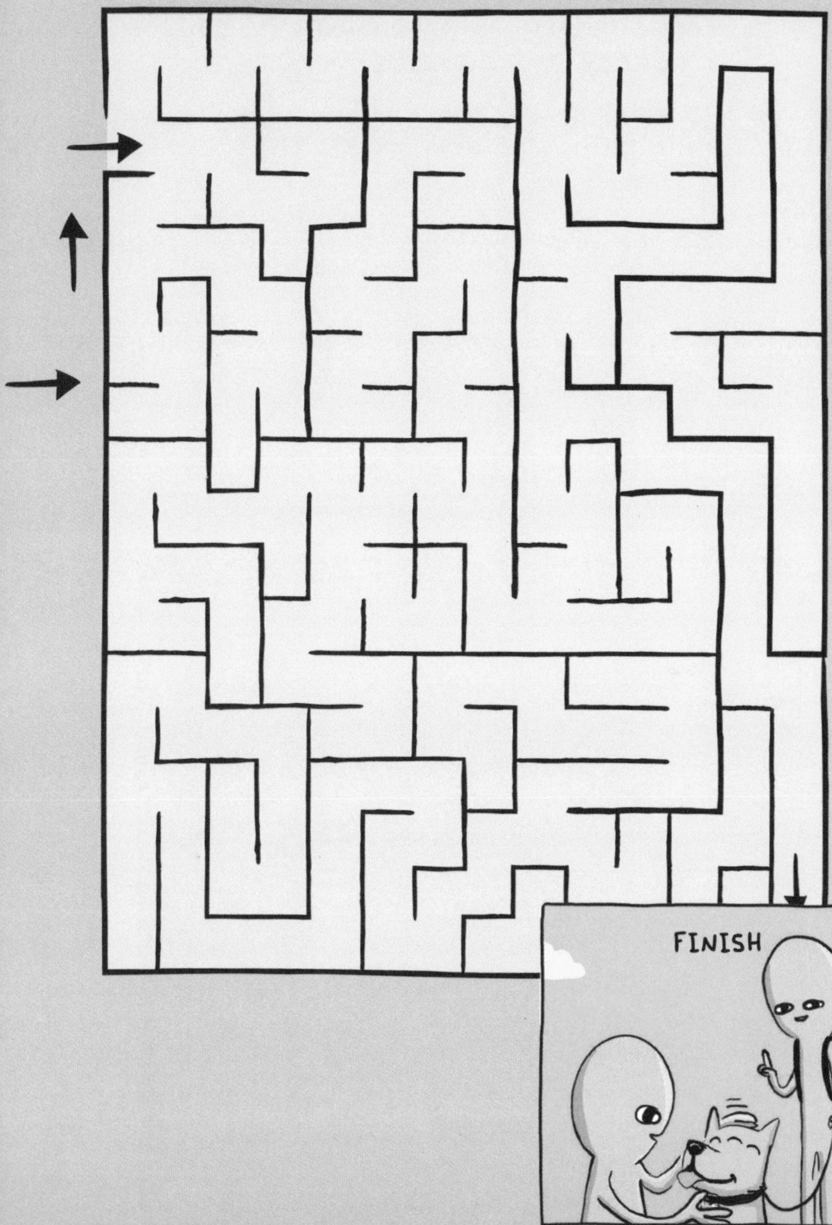
FINISH

FUTILITY AND FATIGUE

TURN THE STEPS INTO MILES AND CIRCLE THE LONGEST RUN.

1600 = ________ MILES

4000 = ________ MILES

800 = ________ MILES

3200 = ________ MILES

2400 = ________ MILES

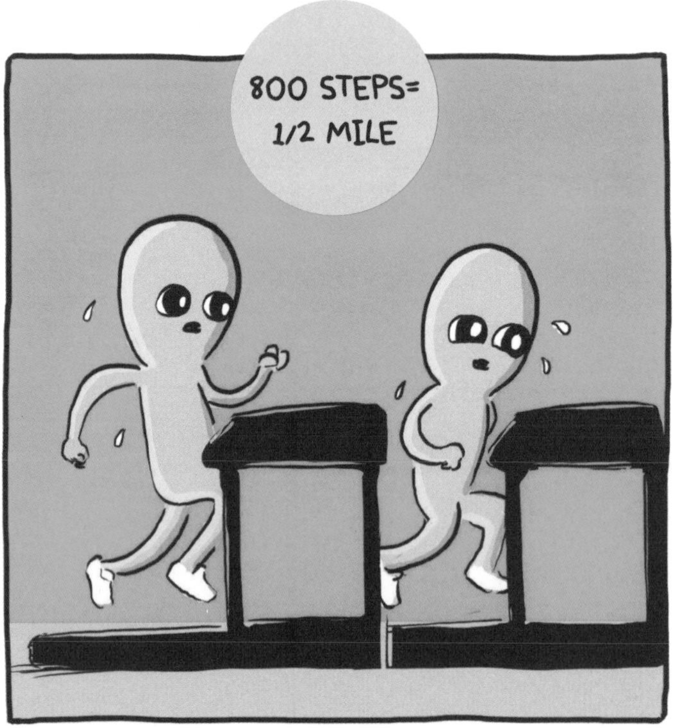
800 STEPS=
1/2 MILE

WHAT HAPPENS NEXT?

FILL IN THE TEXT ON THE NEXT TWO PANELS

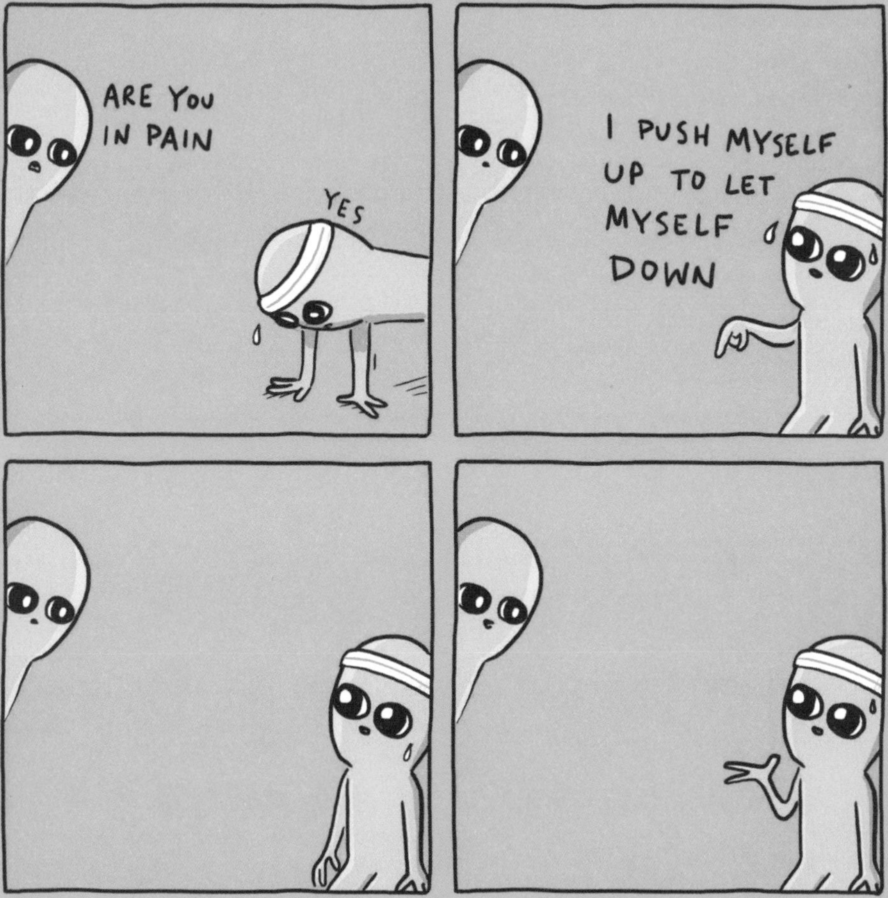
ARE YOU IN PAIN
YES
I PUSH MYSELF UP TO LET MYSELF DOWN

MATCH THE EMOTIONS

WHERE IS YOUR PAIN
IN MY EMOTIONS

WRITE THE WORD BELOW THE PICTURE OF THE MATCHING EMOTION:

SAD

EXCITED

TIRED

RELAXED

GROSSED OUT

SCARED

SMALL EIGHT-LEGGED CREATURE

FILL IN THE BLANKS WITH WORDS FROM THE
BANK TO MAKE A MELODY THAT RHYMES.

WORD BANK OF
RHYMING WORDS:

MAINTAIN

BEFORE

ONCE MORE

DRAIN

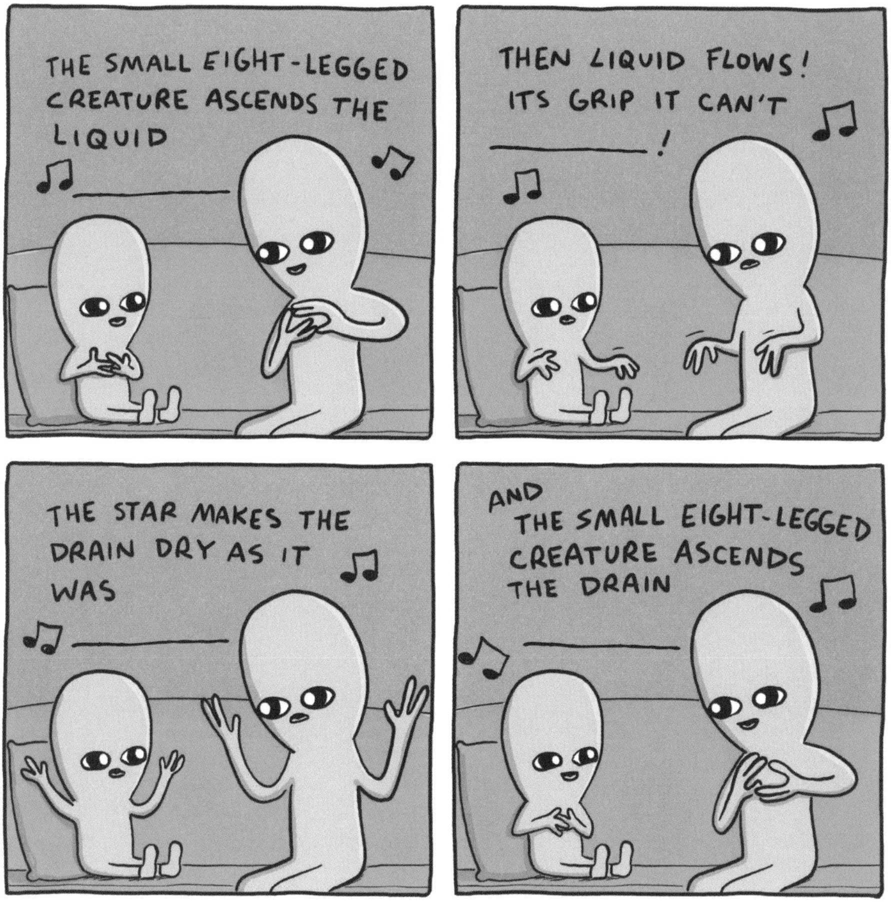
THE SMALL EIGHT-LEGGED CREATURE ASCENDS THE LIQUID
♫ ________ ♫
THEN LIQUID FLOWS! ITS GRIP IT CAN'T ________ ! ♫
♫
THE STAR MAKES THE DRAIN DRY AS IT WAS ♫
♫ ________
AND THE SMALL EIGHT-LEGGED CREATURE ASCENDS THE DRAIN ♫
♫ ________

STABBING SWEET CUSHIONS

FILL IN THE MISSING NUMBER PATTERNS IN THE SWEET CUSHIONS.

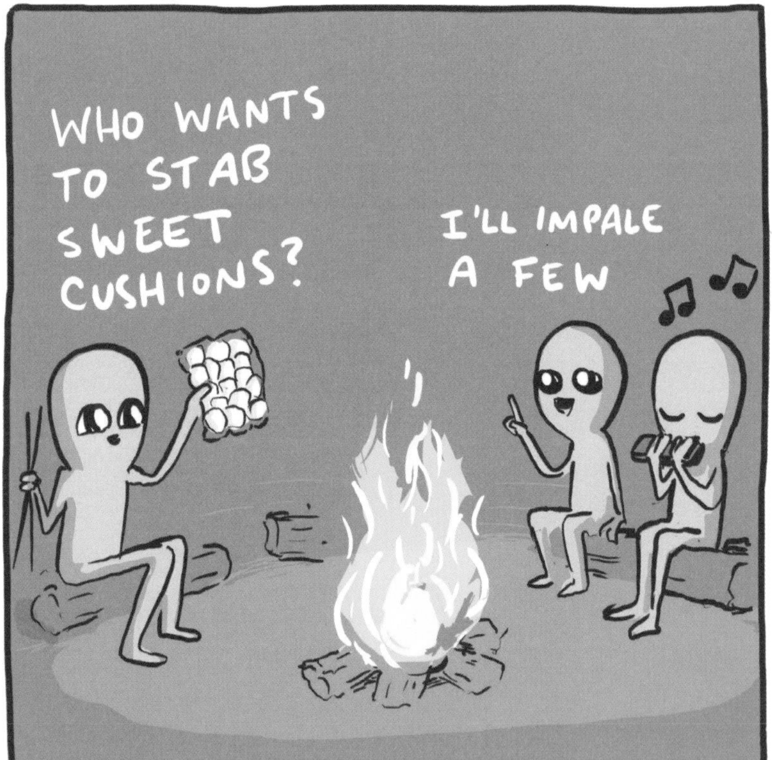

WHO WANTS TO STAB SWEET CUSHIONS?
I'LL IMPALE A FEW

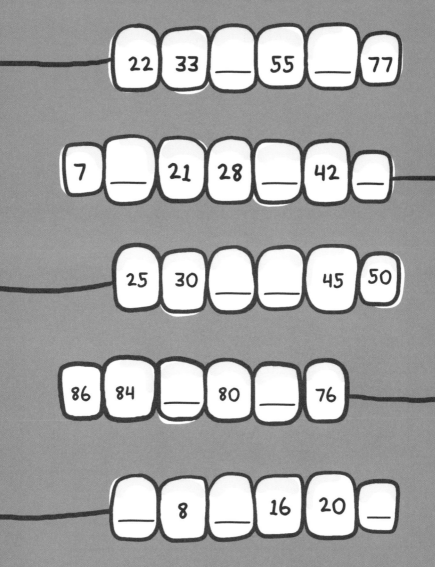

22　33　___　55　___　77

7　___　21　28　___　42　___

25　30　___　___　45　50

86　84　___　80　___　76

___　8　___　16　20　___

ASSESS YOUR FEAR
CIRCLE THE WORDS THAT
MEAN THE OPPOSITE
OF "BRAVE."

BOLD

SCARED

HEROIC

SPOOKED

TIMID

TERRIFIED

CALM

HAPPY

FEARLESS

FRIGHTENED

WHISPER A REQUEST TO A GASEOUS ORB

SOLVE THE PUZZLE TO FIND OUT THE
LAST LINE OF THE SONG.

$\overline{I}\ \overline{G}\ \overline{T}$ $\overline{K}\ \overline{C}\ \overline{N}\ \overline{N}$

$\overline{E}\ \overline{S}\ \overline{A}\ \overline{S}\ \overline{C}\ \overline{P}\ \overline{S}$

A=C S=E G=O E=R T=U

K=W N=L I=Y C=I P=V

MODERATELY HAZARDOUS WILDERNESS MULTIPLICATION

ANSWER THE MULTIPLICATION PROBLEMS TO CLIMB OVER THE MOUNTAIN.

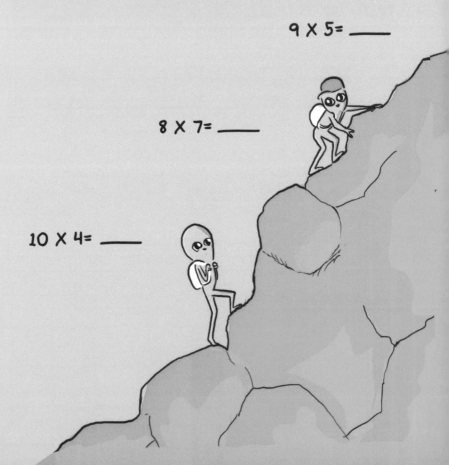

$9 \times 5 = $ _____

$8 \times 7 = $ _____

$10 \times 4 = $ _____

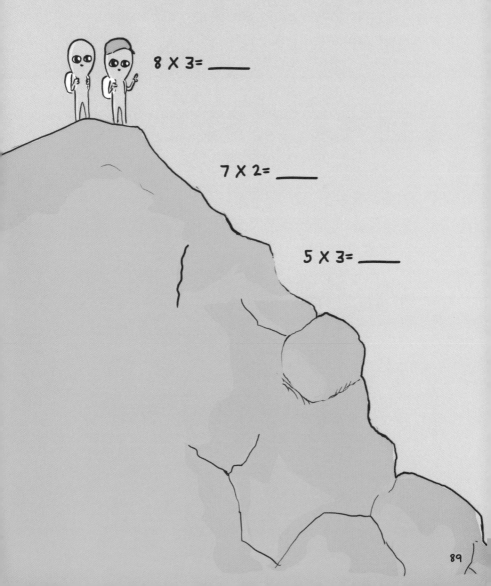

8 X 3 = _____

7 X 2 = _____

5 X 3 = _____

NATURE WITH REGULATIONS

CREATE A LOW-DETAIL RENDERING OF A PARK WITH A PLAYGROUND.

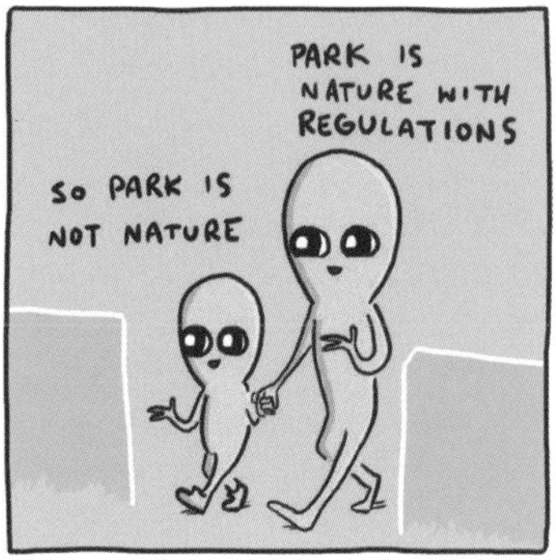
PARK IS NATURE WITH REGULATIONS
SO PARK IS NOT NATURE

MATCH THE OBJECT NAME WITH THE IMAGE.

SERIOUSNESS CLOTH

FOOT RAMPS

STAND-UP RINSE OFF

RECREATIONAL FACE-STRIKING HANDCOVER

GROUP ROLLMACHINE

BEHIND-BAG

WILDLY UNPREPARED MAZE

ASSIST THE BEING FROM THE RAIN
TO THE SKYSHIELD.

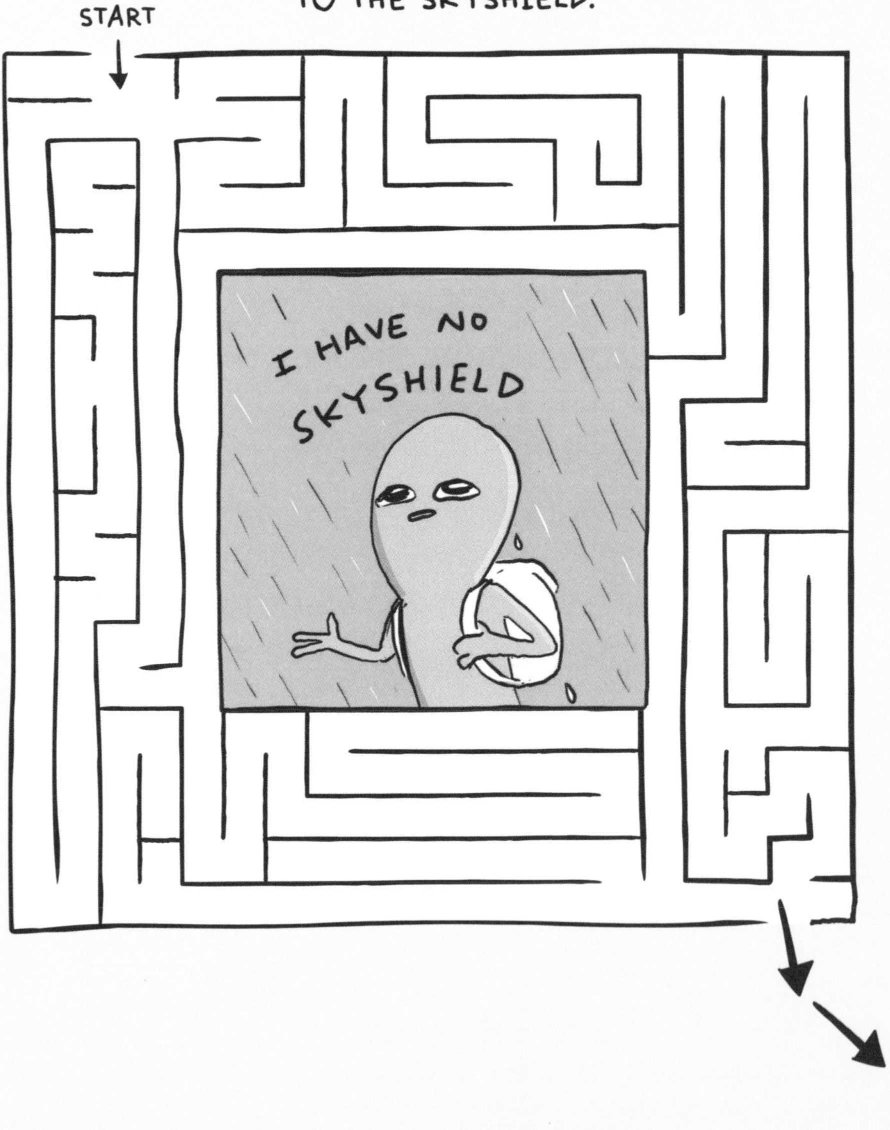
START
I HAVE NO SKYSHIELD

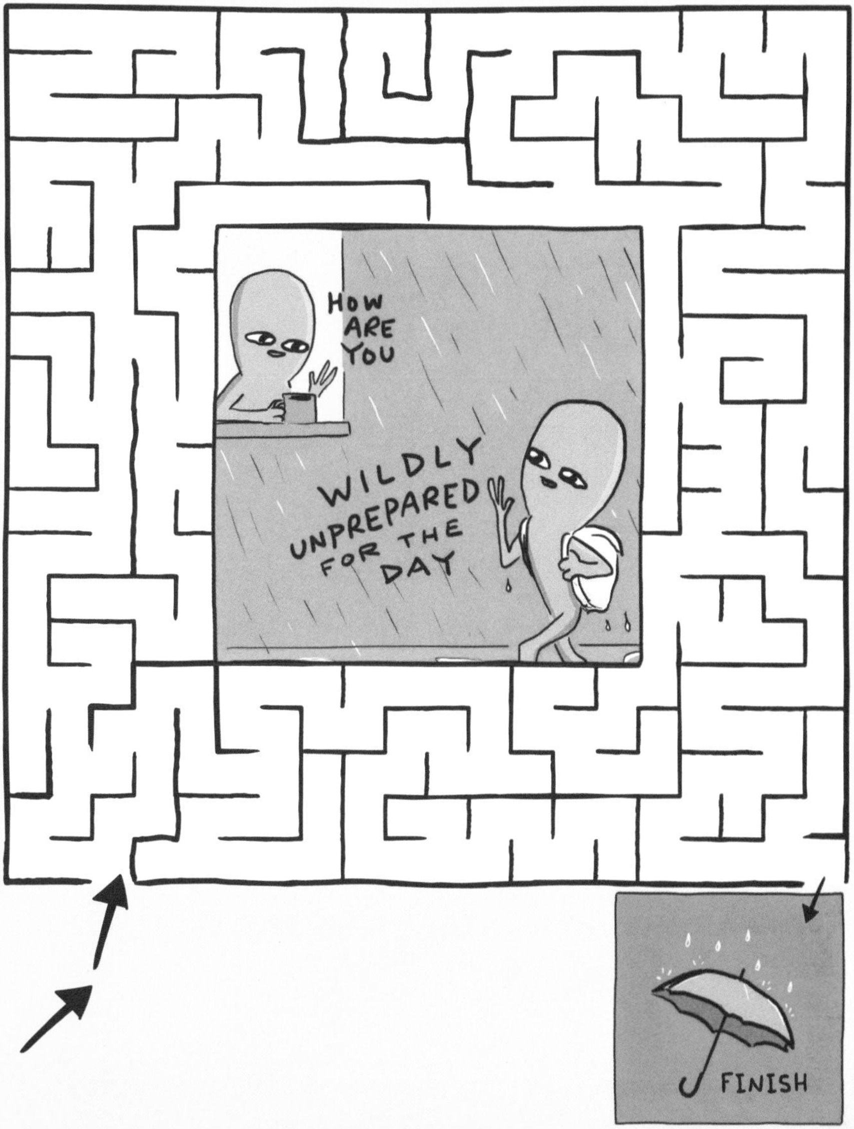

HOW ARE YOU
WILDLY UNPREPARED FOR THE DAY
FINISH

TIME TO BE FULLY CONSCIOUS

TIME TO BE FULLY CONSCIOUS
I REQUEST A SMALL EXTENSION
REQUEST DENIED
A FEW MORE TIME INCREMENTS
ILLUMINATING YOUR REST CHAMBER
A ONE PERCENT REST INCREA-
CREATING A SMALLER CHAMBER
I ADMIT THAT WAS RESOURCEFUL

DRAW HANDS ON THE CLOCK TO SHOW THE TIME YOU:

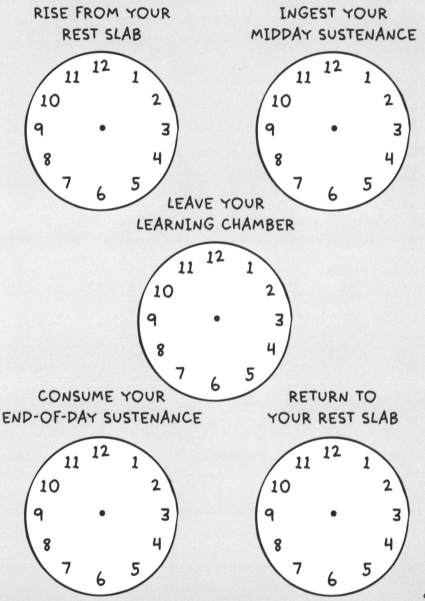

RISE FROM YOUR
REST SLAB

INGEST YOUR
MIDDAY SUSTENANCE

LEAVE YOUR
LEARNING CHAMBER

CONSUME YOUR
END-OF-DAY SUSTENANCE

RETURN TO
YOUR REST SLAB

TINY TRASH SEEK AND FIND

CIRCLE THE BEINGS YOU FIND IN THE TINY TRASH.

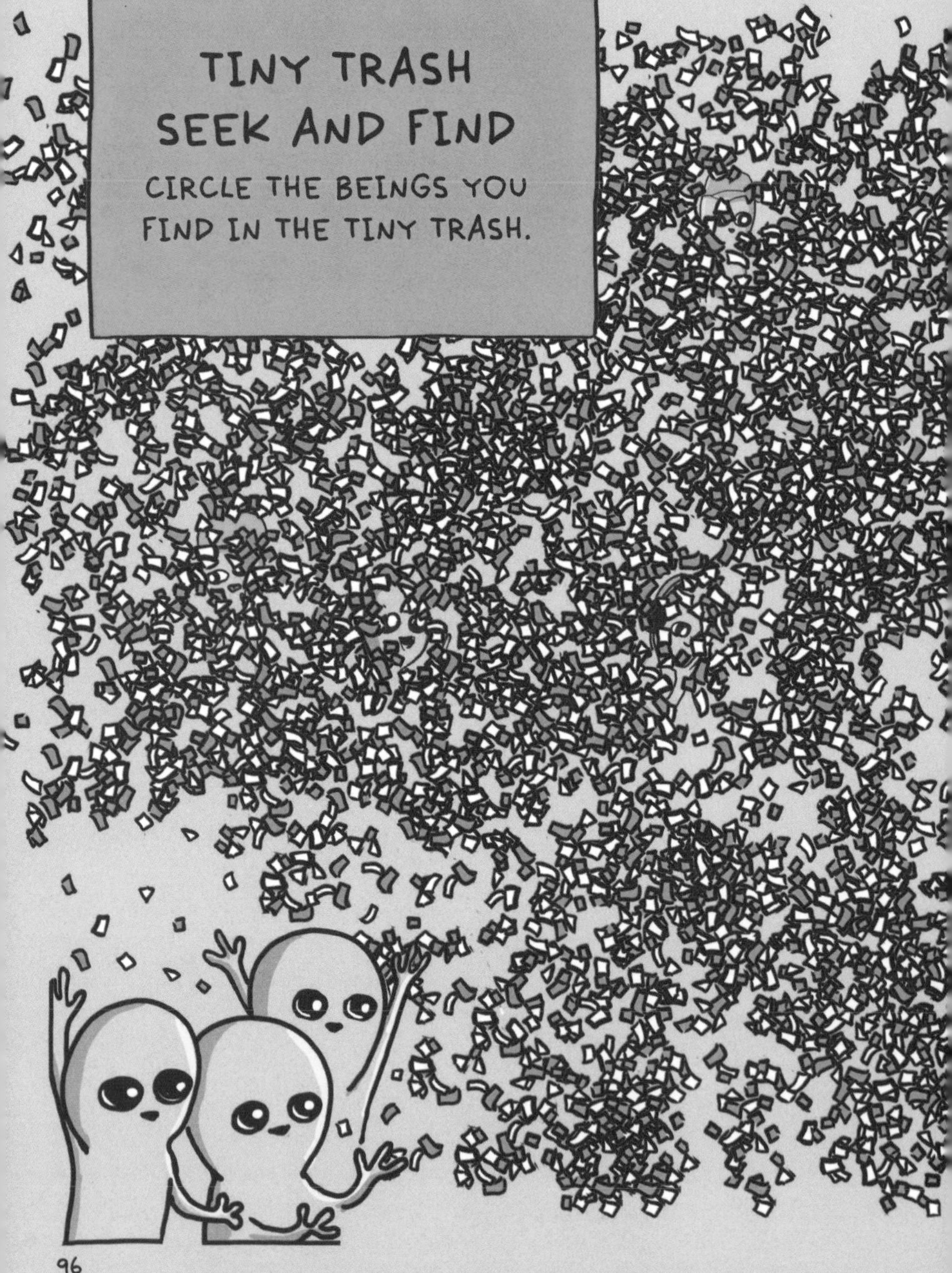

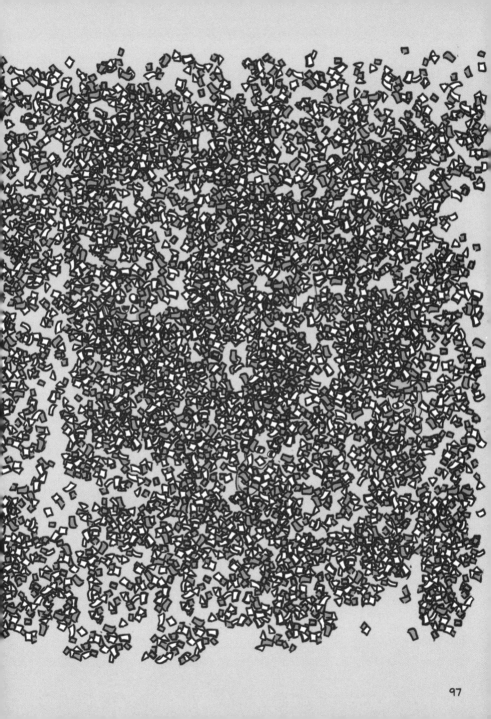

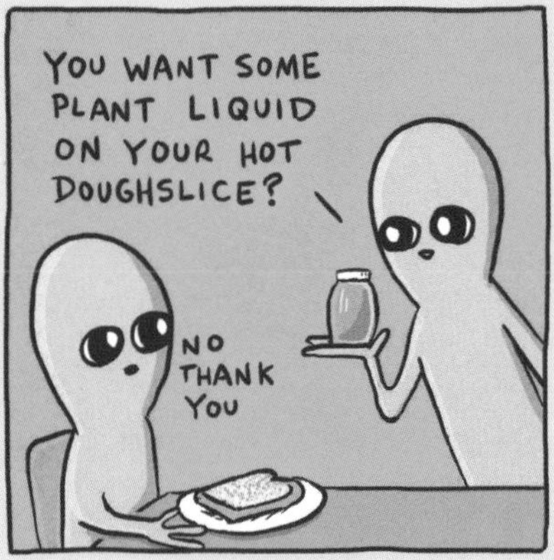
YOU WANT SOME PLANT LIQUID ON YOUR HOT DOUGHSLICE?
NO THANK YOU

TWICE HEATBLASTED DOUGHSLICE

SEARCH FOR WORDS FOUND IN YOUR MORNING SUSTENANCE.

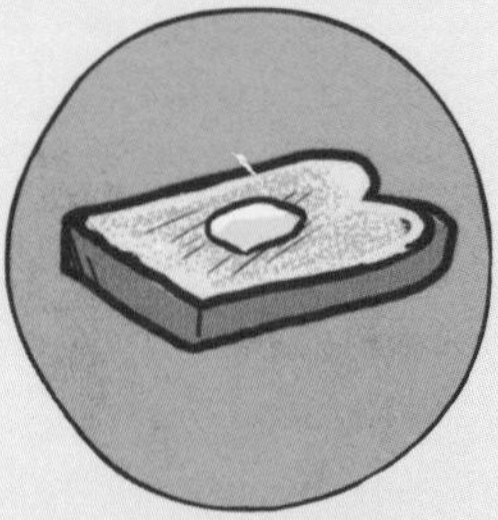

HOT DOUGHSLICE

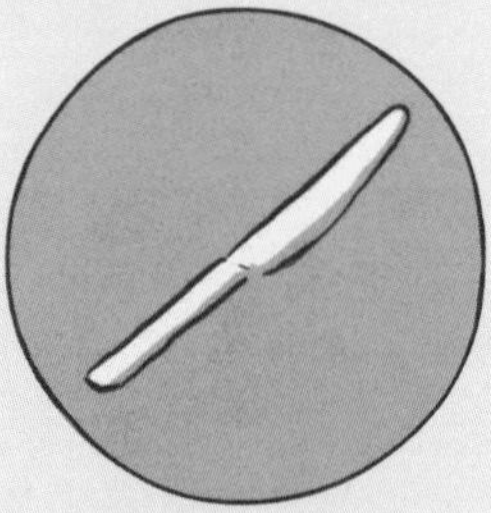

SLICER

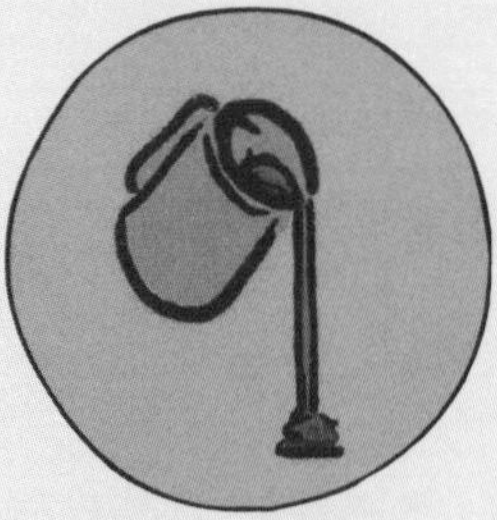

SWEET SAUCE

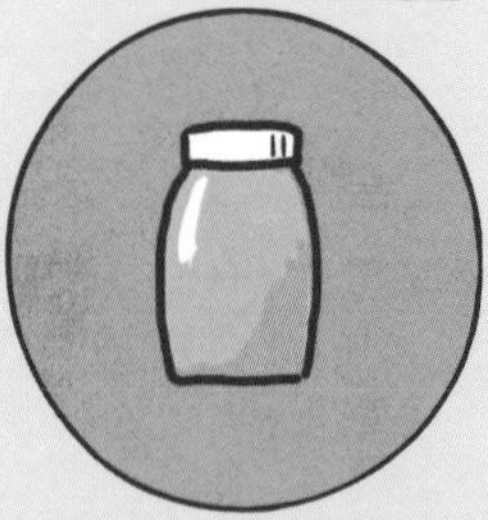

PLANT LIQUID

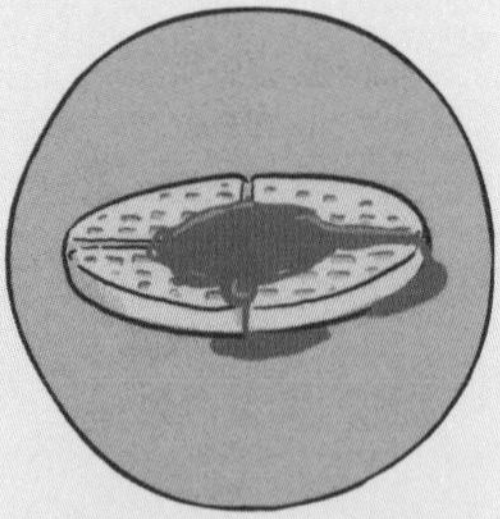

CRISS-CROSS FLOPPER

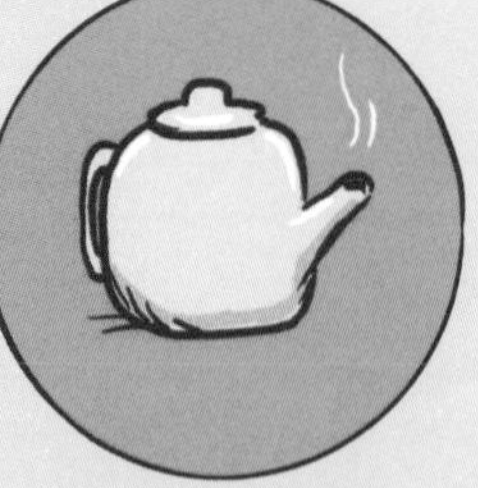

HOT LEAF LIQUID

```
F  O  R  C  A  W  T  J  R  F  L  H  M  C  E
Q  H  G  B  P  P  O  E  G  C  L  N  U  L  Y
M  O  X  W  W  B  U  C  U  D  U  C  J  S  P
J  T  E  X  K  N  A  N  W  S  W  R  M  U  F
H  L  D  I  V  E  P  K  S  O  Y  I  J  P  N
O  E  T  I  V  L  I  M  U  W  C  S  Q  H  A
T  A  B  H  U  V  X  O  T  C  T  S  A  V  L
D  F  W  I  A  Q  J  S  K  L  P  C  G  E  W
O  L  S  M  T  Q  I  Q  X  Z  E  R  N  F  Q
U  I  P  L  B  B  W  L  L  K  H  O  F  M  S
G  Q  L  I  E  Y  B  E  T  F  V  S  X  W  F
H  U  D  U  C  C  B  T  S  N  S  S  U  P  S
S  I  S  C  Y  T  U  W  S  A  A  F  L  E  S
L  D  O  H  K  P  N  A  H  M  I  L  K  B  H
I  M  W  C  W  H  T  Z  S  H  B  O  P  J  V
C  J  C  Q  P  D  I  L  S  T  Y  P  D  F  L
E  R  L  R  Z  E  I  B  V  I  E  P  X  P  P
G  Q  U  H  D  C  J  F  W  A  F  E  L  D  D
I  A  P  M  E  Z  G  G  P  U  F  R  W  Y  J
D  Z  A  R  U  C  Q  V  C  Q  T  T  Q  S  L
```

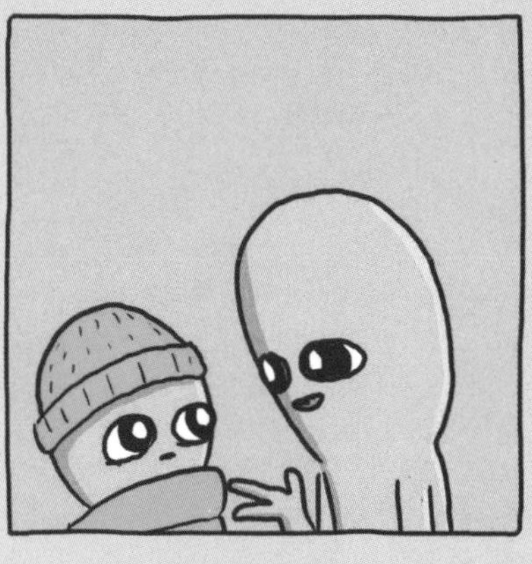

UNPLEASANT ATMOSPHERE

CONNECT THE EVEN NUMBERED DOTS TO FIND A CREATURE SLEEPING IN THE SNOW.

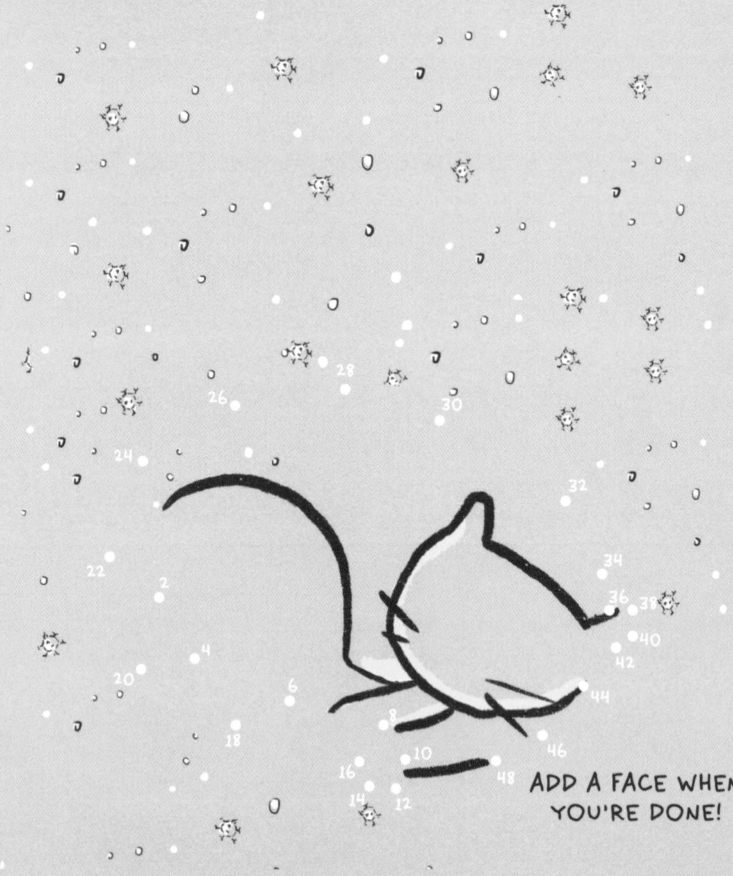

ADD A FACE WHEN YOU'RE DONE!

SLICK-SLAP SCRAMBLE

FILL IN THE BLANKS TO COMPLETE THE WORD.

S _ A _ PE _

_ O O T _ L A _ E S

A _ B I T _ R

S U _ E R _ I _ O _

CRYSTALLIZE FILL-IN-THE-BLANKS

FILL IN THE BLANKS WITH WORDS FROM THE BANK TO MAKE A MELODY THAT RHYMES.

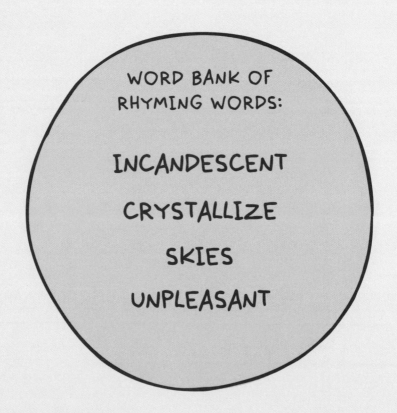

WORD BANK OF
RHYMING WORDS:

INCANDESCENT

CRYSTALLIZE

SKIES

UNPLEASANT

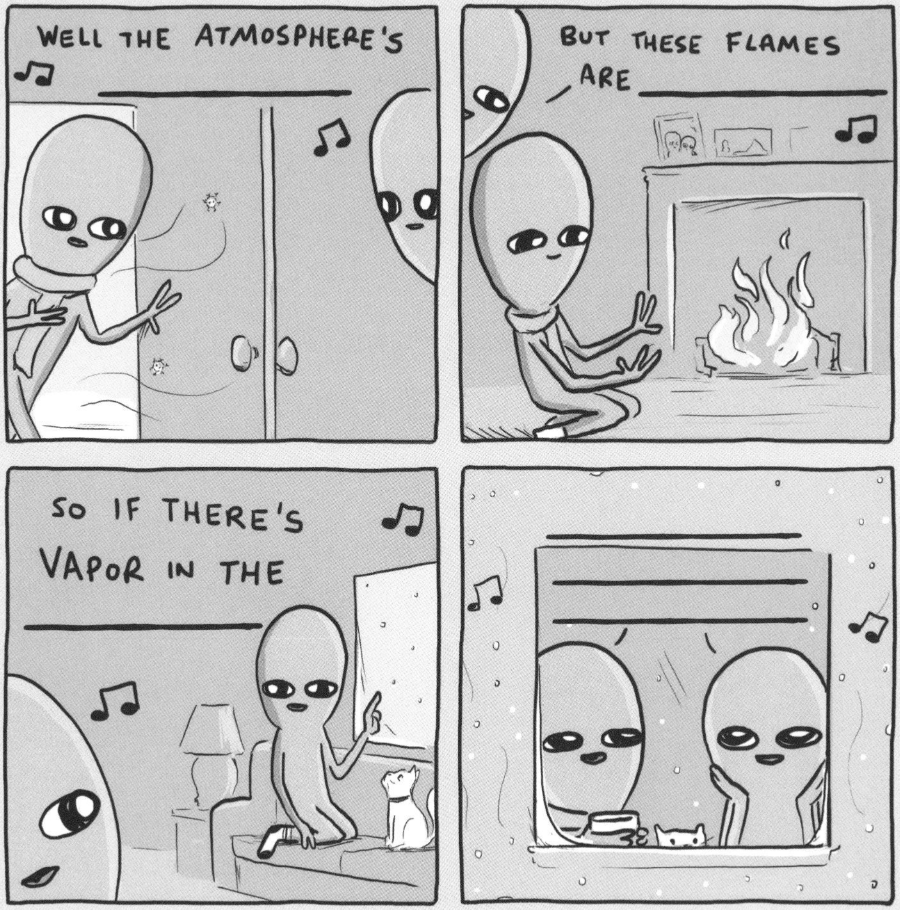
WELL THE ATMOSPHERE'S
BUT THESE FLAMES ARE
SO IF THERE'S VAPOR IN THE

WE CAUGHT THE ORB!
OBSERVE THE DISTINCTION

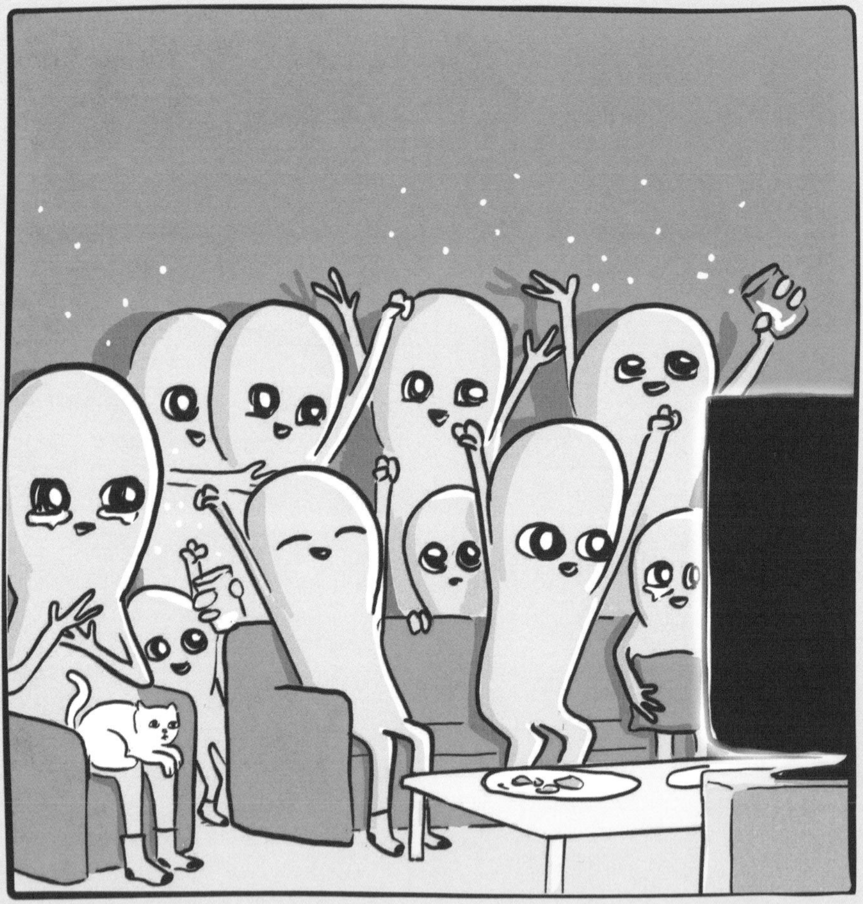

CIRCLE THE 5 DIFFERENCES BETWEEN THE 2 IMAGES.

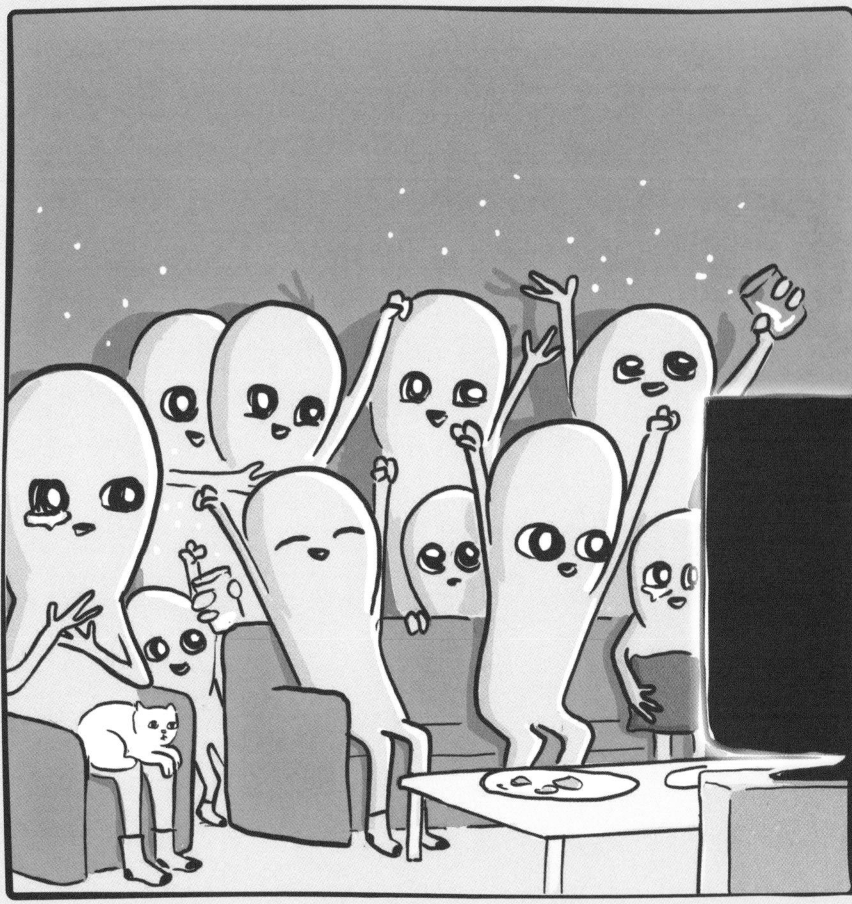

SEARCH FOR SUSTENANCE
DRIVE YOUR ROLL MACHINE
TO FIND SUSTENANCE.

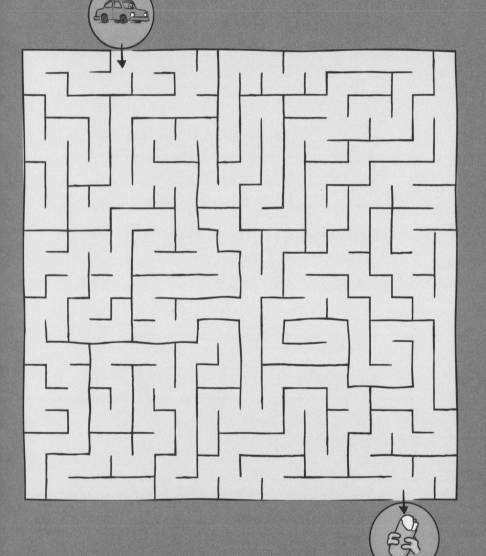

SWEET DISK SUDOKU

CATCH THE CRUMBS BY FILLING IN THE EMPTY SQUARES WITH THE NUMBERS AND SHAPES.

SEE PAGE 66 FOR AN EXAMPLE.

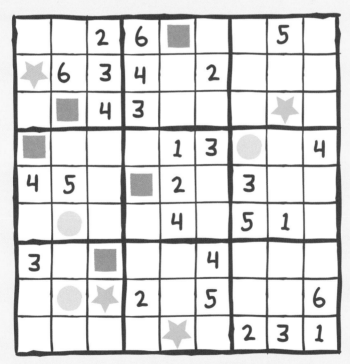

BE SURE TO USE EACH OF THEM JUST ONCE IN EACH ROW AND IN EACH COLUMN.

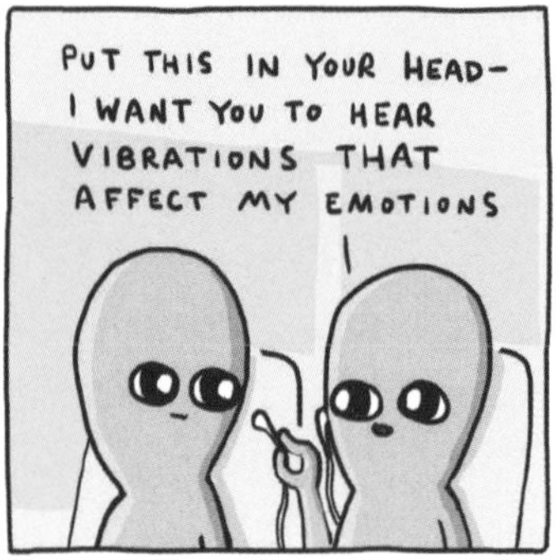
PUT THIS IN YOUR HEAD-
I WANT YOU TO HEAR
VIBRATIONS THAT
AFFECT MY EMOTIONS

VIBRATIONS THAT AFFECT EMOTIONS WORD LADDER

REPLACE LETTERS ON EACH RUNG TO CLIMB TO THE TOP OF THE WORD LADDER.

FINISH

S A N G

CHANGE ONE LETTER. WHEN A MELODY CAME OUT OF YOUR MOUTH.

_ _ _ _

CHANGE TWO LETTERS. WHAT YOU DO WITH YOUR COAT IN A CLOSET.

_ _ _ _

REMOVE TWO LETTERS. WHAT YOU WEAR ON YOUR FINGER.

_ _ _ _ _ _

ADD TWO LETTERS. YOU NEED THIS TO TIE THINGS UP.

S I N G

START

PERFECT SEQUENCE OF MELODIES

CREATE 10 WORDS USING LETTERS FROM THE PHRASE "PERFECT SEQUENCE OF MELODIES."

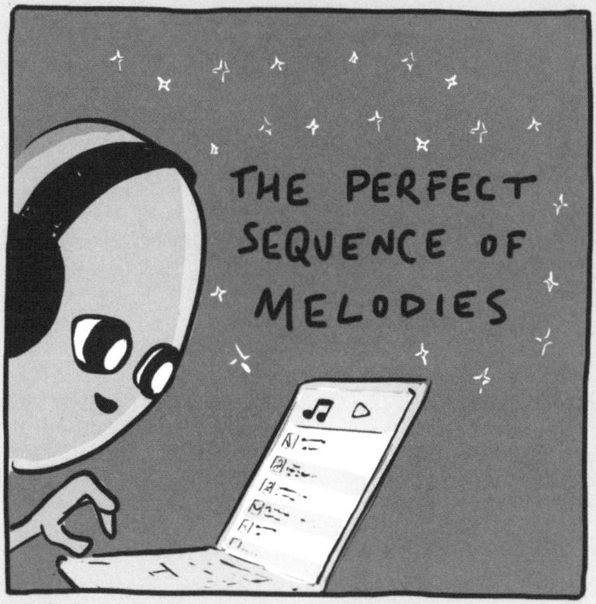
THE PERFECT SEQUENCE OF MELODIES

THE FIRST ONE IS DONE FOR YOU!

1 MUSIC

2 ______

3 ______

4 ______

5 ______

6 ______

7 ______

8 ______

9 ______

10 ______

MELODY MAGIC

DRAW A LINE MATCHING EACH OF THE SAME COLORED NOTES WITHOUT CROSSING THE LINES. THERE'S MORE THAN ONE ANSWER.

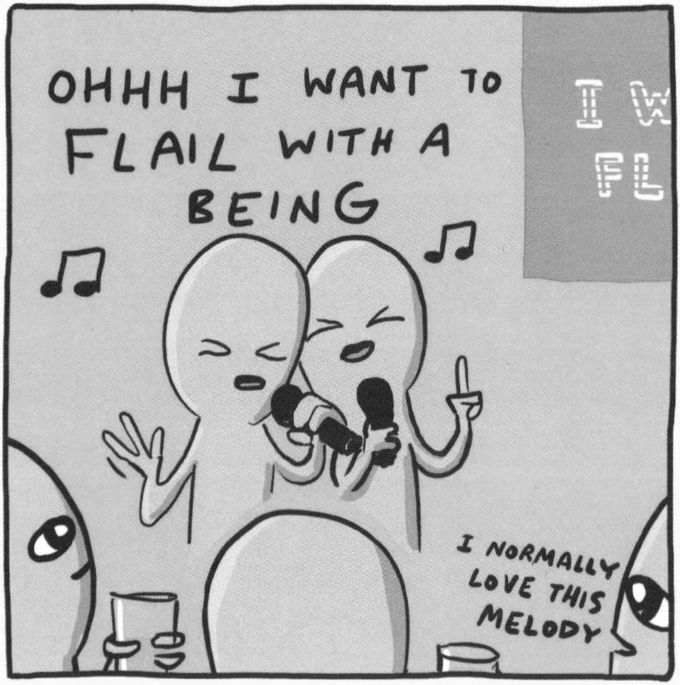
OHHH I WANT TO FLAIL WITH A BEING
I W
FL
I NORMALLY LOVE THIS MELODY

FAREWELL UNSCRAMBLE

$\overline{X}\,\overline{E}\,\overline{V}\,\overline{A}$ $\overline{V}\,\overline{A}$ $\overline{I}\,\overline{E}\,\overline{M}\,\overline{T}\,\overline{M}$

$\overline{I}\,\overline{M}$ $\overline{U}\,\overline{V}\,\overline{S}\,\overline{M}\,\overline{T}\,\overline{L}\,\overline{M}$

I=W	T=R	V=I
M=E	L=G	E=H
U=D	X=T	
S=V	A=S	

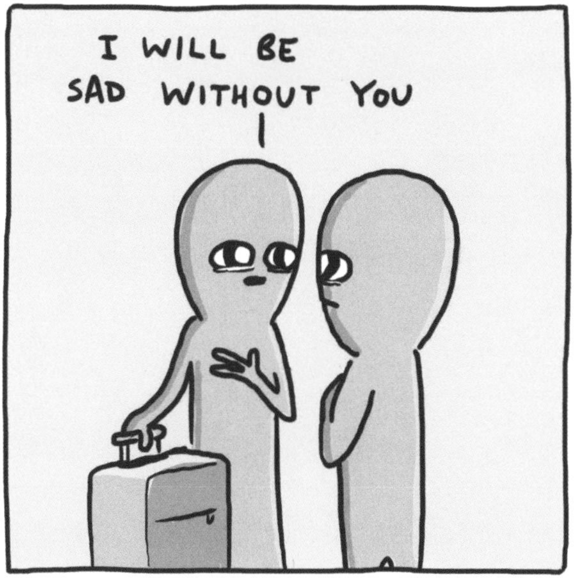
I WILL BE SAD WITHOUT YOU

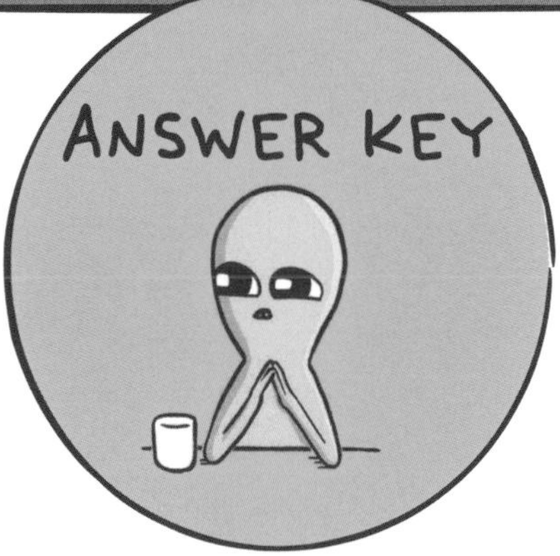
ANSWER KEY

P. 4-5

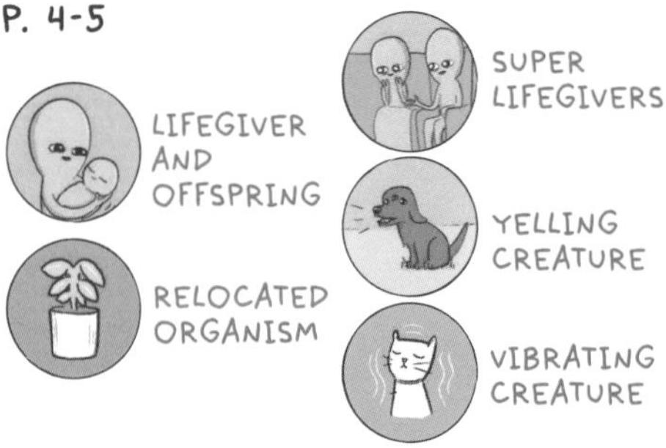
LIFEGIVER AND OFFSPRING
RELOCATED ORGANISM
SUPER LIFEGIVERS
YELLING CREATURE
VIBRATING CREATURE

P. 7

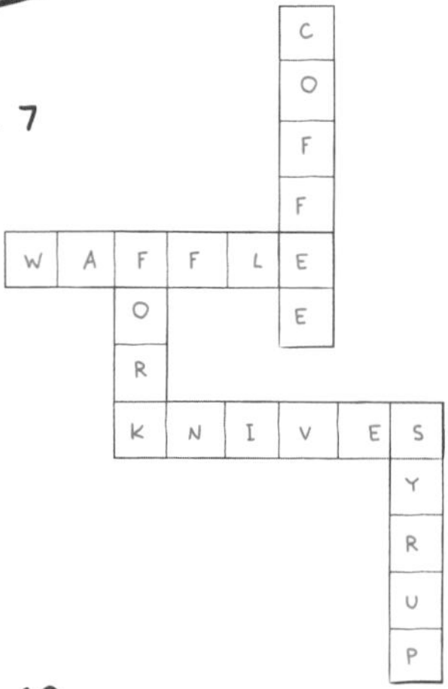
COFFEE
WAFFLE
FORK
KNIVES
SYRUP

P. 8-9

WE NEED OUR STONES TO
BITE AND SHRED,
THIS KEEPS THEM FIRMLY
IN OUR HEAD

RIGHT BEFORE WE REST
OUR BONES,
WE OPEN OUR MOUTHS TO
BRUSH OUR STONES

WE SCRUB UNTIL WE MAKE
THEM SHINE,
AND WHEN WE'RE DONE
WE CAN RECLINE

P. 10

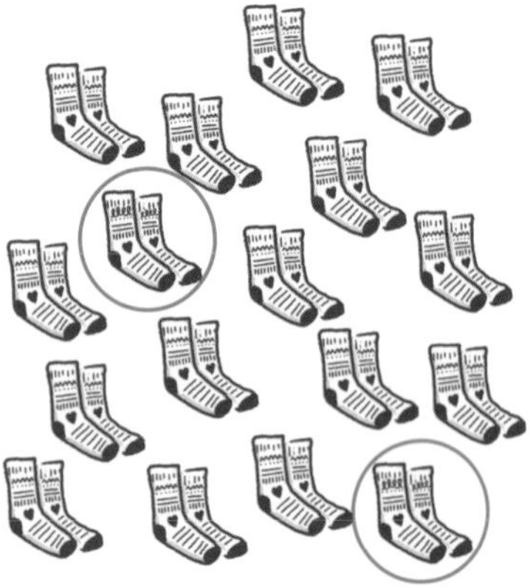

P. 11

MARVELOUS BEING

P. 12

P. 13

P. 14

48" = 4'
42" = 3'6"
54" = 4'6"

P. 15

10, 20, 30, 40, 50, 60
90, 80, 70, 60, 50, 40
10, 20, 40, 80, 160, 320

P. 17

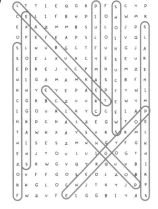

P. 18

LIVING ORGANISM
FOOT-ORB
FLYING CREATURE
FACIAL TOPOGRAPHY KIT
PLANT SCENT LIQUID

P. 23

P. 24

P. 25

IT WENT OVER THEIR HEAD
AIR SLAPPER 7

P. 26

SOCCERBALL
COACH
REFEREE
CLEAT
RULE

P. 27

LET US PUT HANDS TOGETHER
1...2..3
CAN'T USE THESE!

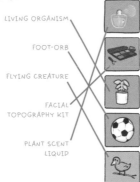

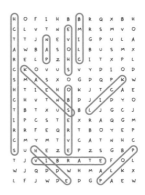

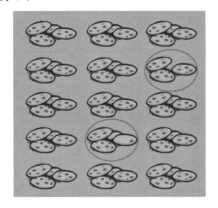

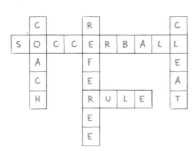

P. 28-29

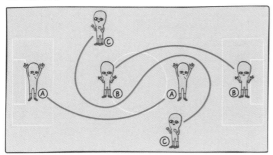

THE REVERSE OF THESE LINES WOULD ALSO BE CORRECT.

P. 31

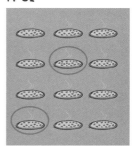

P. 33

P. 34

A = 3
B = 8
C = 2

P. 36

11 + 18 = 29
6 + 13 = 19
10 + 9 = 19
15 + 19 = 34
4 + 14 = 18

P. 39

BEDROOM

STUFFED ANIMAL

BED

CURTAINS

P. 41

IT'S MARVELOUS TO UNDERSTAND
THAT WE HAVE LIQUID ON DEMAND

IT STARTS OUT AT A NATURAL SOURCE
IT TRAVELS WITH IMPRESSIVE FORCE

IT COMES RIGHT OUT WITHOUT DELAY
IT TRANSPORTS ALL OUR FILTH AWAY

OUR USE OF LIQUID IS ADVANCED
AND NOW WE SMELL LIKE LOVELY PLANTS

P. 43

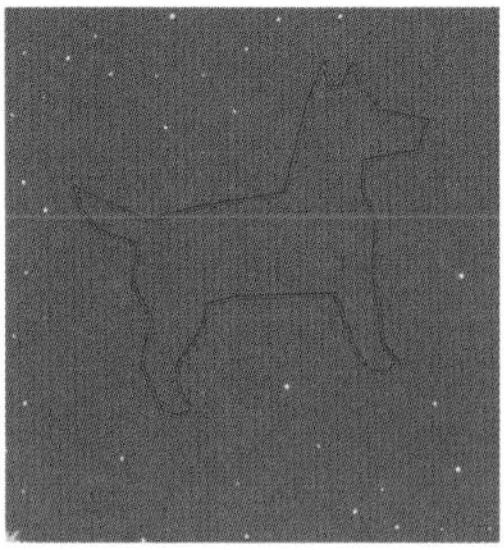

P. 45

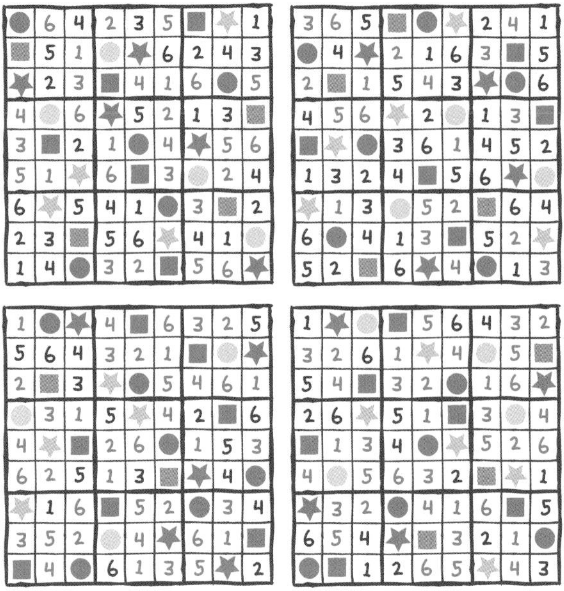

P. 47

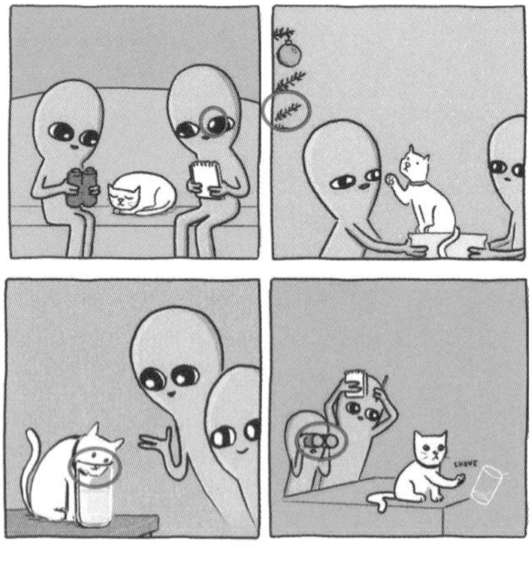
SHOVE

P. 49

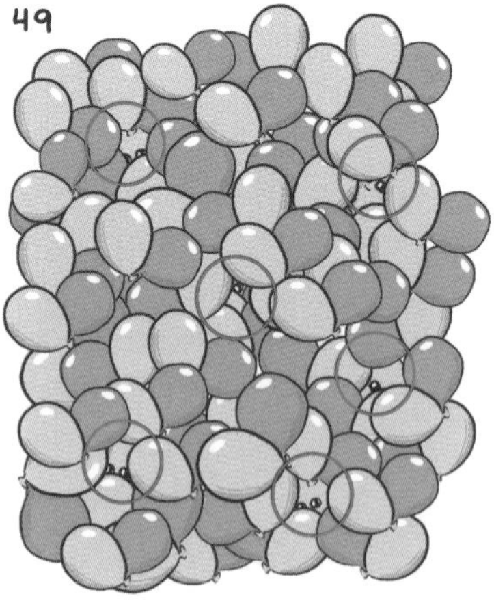

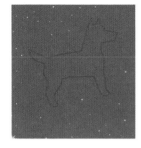

P. 50

$2 \times 2 = 4$ $2 \times 7 = 14$

$2 \times 3 = 6$ $2 \times 8 = 16$

$2 \times 4 = 8$ $2 \times 9 = 18$

$2 \times 5 = 10$ $2 \times 10 = 20$

$2 \times 6 = 12$ $2 \times 11 = 22$

P. 51

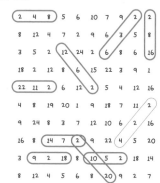

P. 55

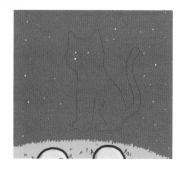

P. 58

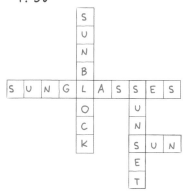

P. 61

P. 63

3	1	5	4	🏀	2	🏈	6	🏀
4	🏈	2	⚽	6	5	1	3	⚾
6	🏀	🏐	1	🏈	3	2	4	5
⚽	2	3	🏈	1	6	5	🏀	4
🏈	6	4	2	5	🏐	⚽	1	3
5	🏐	1	3	⚽	4	6	🏈	2
🏀	5	⚽	6	3	1	4	2	🏈
2	3	6	5	4	🏈	🏀	⚽	1
1	4	🏈	🏀	2	⚽	3	5	6

4	3	🏈	2	6	⚽	🏐	1	5
6	🏀	⚽	4	5	1	2	3	🏈
1	5	2	🏈	3	🏀	⚽	4	6
🏐	🏈	4	3	1	2	6	5	🏀
🏀	1	5	6	4	🏈	3	🏐	2
3	2	6	⚽	🏀	5	1	🏈	4
5	🏀	3	🏐	🏈	6	4	2	1
2	4	1	5	🏀	3	🏈	6	🏐
🏈	6	🏐	1	2	4	5	🏀	3

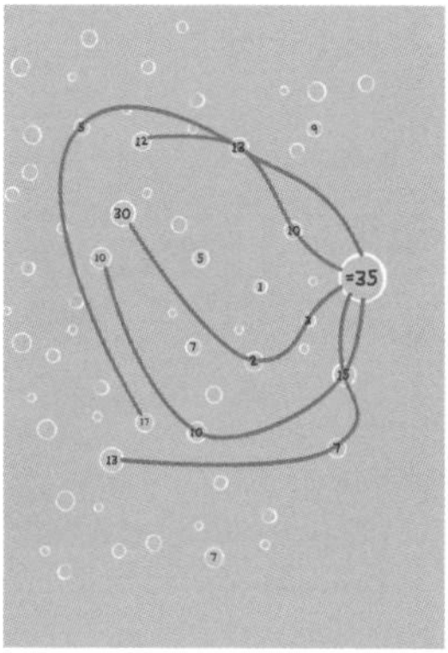

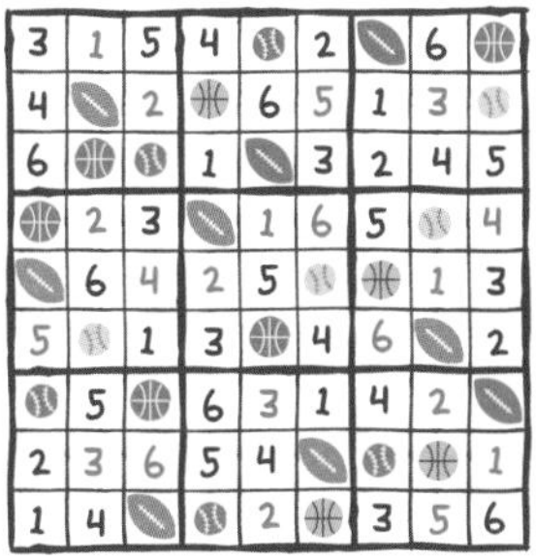

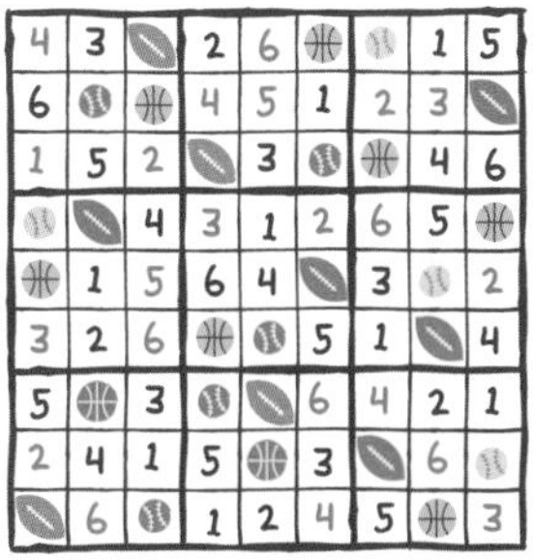

P. 65

WE DID
NOT DIE

P. 67

W I N G

W I N D

B I N D

B I R D

P. 68

P. 71

I SENSE WE MISREAD THE INSTRUCTIONS
ACCURATE

P. 72

OBSCURE-AND-PURSUE	HERE I COME
I AM APPROACHING	READY OR NOT
RESTRICTING MY VISION	HIDE-AND-SEEK
PREPARED OR NOT	COVER MY EYES

P. 73

OBSCURE-AND-PURSUE (HIDE-AND-SEEK)

P. 74

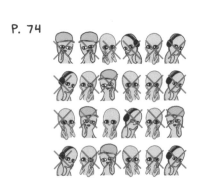

P. 75

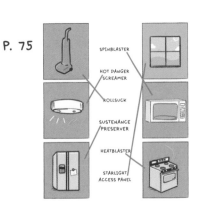

SPINBLASTER
HOT DANGER SCREAMER
ROLLSUCK
SUSTENANCE PRESERVER
HEATBLASTER
STARLIGHT ACCESS PANEL

P. 76-77

P. 78

1600 = __1__ MILES

4000 = __2.5__ MILES

800 = __1/2__ MILES

3200 = __2__ MILES

2400 = __1.5__ MILES

P. 81

GROSSED EXCITED
OUT

TIRED    SAD

SCARED  RELAXED

P. 83

THE SMALL EIGHT-LEGGED CREATURE
ASCENDS THE LIQUID DRAIN

THEN LIQUID FLOWS!
ITS GRIP IT CAN'T MAINTAIN

THE STAR MAKES THE DRAIN DRY AS IT
WAS BEFORE

AND THE SMALL EIGHT-LEGGED CREATURE
ASCENDS THE DRAIN ONCE MORE

P. 85

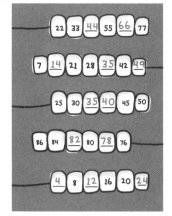

22 33 44 55 66 77

7 14 21 28 35 42 49

25 30 35 40 45 50

86 84 82 80 78 76

4 8 12 16 20 24

P. 86

BOLD SCARED

HEROIC SPOOKED

TIMID TERRIFIED

CALM

HAPPY

FEARLESS FRIGHTENED

P. 87

YOU WILL RECEIVE

P. 88-89

8 x 3 = 24
9 x 5 = 45
7 x 2 = 14
8 x 7 = 56
5 x 3 = 15
10 x 4 = 40

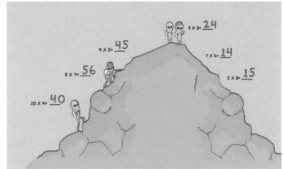

P. 91

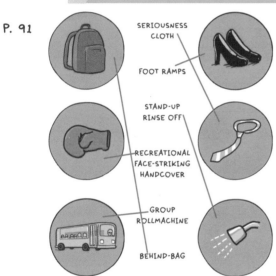

SERIOUSNESS CLOTH
FOOT RAMPS
STAND-UP RINSE OFF
RECREATIONAL FACE-STRIKING HANDCOVER
GROUP ROLLMACHINE
BEHIND-BAG

P. 92-93

I HAVE NO SKYSHIELD
HOW ARE YOU
WILDLY UNPREPARED FOR THE DAY